'I don't ca  **said. 'Or wh**

As long as we're

He didn't say it, but it seemed so clear.

'Neither do I…' Emma's heart gave its usual giddy lurch in her chest, and she wanted his company so badly that she almost felt ill.

The hospital was so quiet this time of night. Visitors and most doctors had gone home. The two of them were alone.

'My place, then,' she added shakily.

They left the building together and walked in the direction of the car park. Pete put his arm around her, drawing her close to his side, and for a moment she let her head dip onto his shoulder.

It felt too good. She lifted her head again and slid out of the circle of his arm. He let her go without protest, as if he hadn't wanted more. They both knew quite definitely, however, that he had.

Medical Romance™ is proud to present
an emotionally gripping duet by talented author

Lilian Darcy

Katherine and Emma are midwives
at a busy maternity unit in
GLENFALLON HOSPITAL.

Glenfallon is a large rural community
in the beautiful wine-making region of
New South Wales, Australia.

Also in the duet is Katherine's story:
The Midwife's Courage—on sale November 2003.

And later, in 2004, look out for more
Glenfallon Hospital stories!

THE HONOURABLE MIDWIFE

BY
LILIAN DARCY

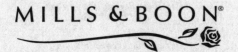

MILLS & BOON®

First published in Great Britain 2003
Harlequin Mills & Boon Limited,
Eton House, 18-24 Paradise Road, Richmond, Surrey TW9 1SR

© Lilian Darcy 2003

ISBN 0 263 83487 5

Set in Times Roman 10½ on 12 pt.
03-1203-48168

Printed and bound in Spain
by Litografia Rosés, S.A., Barcelona

CHAPTER ONE

THERE was bound to be something left behind, Pete Croft decided as he walked around Emma Burns's house and garden one last time. A toy hidden under a flower-pot during a game and then forgotten, or some stray coins in a drawer.

No, there'd be more than that. Something much more personal. Something that would endure for longer.

He stood on the back veranda and looked at the garden. It was the start of spring, the first weekend of September, and there were daffodils and blossom trees and golden acacias in bloom.

The grass was a lush green, and he'd mowed it just this morning, so that the fresh, earthy scent of the clippings still hung in the air. He could hear a couple of other motor mowers going in the distance, too. It was a weekend sound, a hopeful sound, and somehow more soothing to the spirits than such a sound had any right to be.

Inside Emma's house, cool polished floorboards gleamed, and spring sunshine made the living room bright. On any other Saturday, Pete might have stretched out on that squishy-cushioned regency-stripe couch with the weekend city newspaper and a cup of good coffee. Today, however, he had to move out.

I don't want to leave, he realised.

He'd been happy here, during the three-month inter-lude of his tenancy. He'd found a tranquillity and peace he'd never known in quite the same way before, and an

5

odd kind of friendship, via e-mail, with his temporary landlady on the other side of the world in France.

These were the things he didn't want to leave behind. The sheer tranquillity. Emma's e-mails. The sense of her personality lingering like a well-loved fragrance in every room. The sight of his four-year-old twin daughters playing in their 'cubby house' under the old hydrangea bushes, without an apparent care in the world, despite the upheaval unleashed on them by the collapsing of their parents' marriage.

His marriage. His marriage to Claire.

This was the reason Pete made another tour through the house. He went down the brick steps at the front, around the slate paved path at the side of the house and into the back garden once more, rebelling against a reality he couldn't change.

He didn't want to leave at all.

But, of course, he had to. Emma Burns was coming home tomorrow, after her three-month trip, and he was moving into his own brand-new place in Glenfallon's trendiest suburban housing development. The interlude had to end, and real life had to resume.

He'd had professional cleaners in, and he'd groomed Emma's garden himself. The fact that it was spring and flowers were in bloom made it a little easier than it would otherwise have been for him to tell the real plants from the weeds.

The real estate agent was dropping in this afternoon to satisfy himself that everything was in order, but Pete knew this was just a formality. Everything was in order. There was really nothing more to do. He put the key in an envelope, along with a card he'd written to Emma, left them on the kitchen bench top, let himself out the front door and clicked it shut behind him.

*   *   *

Dr Croft had left a couple of things, Emma discovered on Sunday afternoon. The card, for one, which was nice. It was thick and expensive, with a lushly colourful painting of poppies on the front. Inside, he'd written, 'Welcome home, and thanks for renting me your little slice of paradise at a time when I really needed it, Pete. P. S. I want the names of your paint colours.'

His e-mails had been like that, too. Simple and brief, most of them, they'd bounced from heartfelt to practical and back again in the space of three sentences. She had replied in the same vein, and several times over the past three months they'd had a conversation going back and forth for days—a conversation which had had nothing to do with the impersonal tenant-to-landlady issue that had begun it.

Standing in her empty, pristine kitchen, Emma smiled.

She'd enjoyed those electronic conversations. She'd enjoyed the fact that she'd been sitting in an internet café in Paris, with half a dozen languages chittering around her. She'd enjoyed feeling tired and hot, and she'd enjoyed smelling of sugar and cheese and chocolate after hours of lessons in haute cuisine.

Most of all, oddly enough, she'd enjoyed the companionship. On a professional level, she'd known Pete Croft on and off for…well, it had to be several years, at least, but it had taken flurries of e-mails flashing back and forth across half the world to make her feel as if she knew him as a person.

E-mails, and the fact that he'd been living in her house.

Emma was tired and jet-lagged after the long flight from Europe and the connecting hop, in a small propellor-driven aircraft, from Sydney to Glenfallon. The ground didn't seem quite steady beneath her feet. There was a lot to do if she was going to get settled back in before she started work on Tuesday, but she found it impossible to put her flagging energy to anything useful just yet.

Instead, she wandered around the house and garden, finding evidence of her tenant's recent occupation. He'd repaired the latch on the side gate, and the torn flyscreen on the kitchen door. His four-year-old twin daughters, Jessie and Zoe, had dropped a brown Lego horse in the daffodil bed.

He'd left a bottle of brand-new aftershave on the bathroom window-sill, hidden behind a set of cheap lace curtains which she intended to replace soon. For some reason, Emma was tempted to open the aftershave, to see if it smelled like him—What, could it smell like his e-mails?—but sensibly she didn't. She would give it and the Lego horse back to him when she got a chance, but doubted the matter was urgent.

She knew Pete had bought a house in the new development at the edge of town, but didn't have the address. He would be busy moving in, finalising the details of his divorce, his property settlement and his custody arrangements. Plastic horses and missing bottles of unused aftershave would be far, far down on his list of priorities.

'I'll unpack, and put on a load of laundry, and get myself organised,' Emma decided, and wondered if it was only because her wonderful three months in Paris was over that she felt so flat.

'Dr Croft? It's Patsy McNichol.'

'Yes, Patsy? What is it?'

Pete blinked, rubbed the sleep out of his eyes and tried to lift his voice above its early-morning creak. The red figures on the clock radio beside his bed showed six twenty-five, and it was not yet fully light. He was quickly alert, however. He knew this patient wouldn't be phoning him at such an hour on a whim.

'I'm bleeding again,' she said. 'But it's much worse, this time, and…and there's some cramping, too.'

'What kind of cramping?'

'Well, I don't know. Could it be contractions?' She was trying to keep her voice steady, but it wasn't working. Pete could hear the wobble and the pitch of panic. She didn't want this to be happening yet.

'How does the pain feel, Patsy? Is it steady? Describe it for me.'

'It sort of drags, like really bad menstrual cramps, but it's tight, too. It builds, and then it ebbs, and then a little while later—I should have been timing it, shouldn't I?— it builds again. It woke me up about half an hour ago, and I just lay there, but then I felt the blood.'

'How much?'

'The bed is soaked.'

'Is it still flowing?'

'It's eased off. Seems to have.'

'Are you lying down?'

'Yes, with my feet up.'

'Can Brian drive you to the hospital?'

'We're already dressed. I didn't want to disturb you any earlier than I had to.'

Pete dammed back a sigh of frustration. Why were people like this? He had patients who would phone his home number at midnight, complaining of a paper cut, without so much as a 'Sorry to bother you', and patients who would hang back on a lifesaving call in order to give him ten minutes more sleep.

'I'll see you there as soon as I can,' he told Patsy.

He dressed quickly, opting for a set of green surgical gear—drawstring pants and a short-sleeved, V-necked top. Realistically, given the position and size of Patsy's uterine fibroids, he was probably going to be assisting with an emergency Caesarean first thing this morning.

He could feel the aridity of his new bedroom as he moved around it in the early-morning light. The whole house was still far too bare and echoing and new after the cottage cosiness and warmth of Emma Burns's place, which he'd been forced to abandon three days ago.

How did you achieve that sort of atmosphere? he wondered. He wasn't convinced he had the skills, or the time. Well, certainly not the latter. So much on his plate right now.

Claire's behaviour was like a nightmare. Her ultimatums to him didn't make sense. He suspected she was sleeping around, but perhaps that wasn't fair. Perhaps he was simply displacing the real sources of his anger onto a safer issue. How well was she looking after the girls? He wasn't happy with their informal custody arrangement as it stood. He wanted more involvement in his daughters' lives.

And now Patsy McNichol had apparently gone into premature labour, with bleeding that didn't surprise him but definitely wasn't good. She'd done well so far with the pregnancy, and they'd all been crossing their fingers that this wouldn't happen.

There was no time to eat, or to gulp the coffee he craved. He left a message on the answering-machine at his practice, asking his staff to reschedule the first hour of his morning appointments, and he reversed out of the garage and pressed his finger to the button on his remote control garage door opener at six thirty-three.

He couldn't help reviewing Patsy McNichol's history

as he drove. She was thirty-five years old, by no means
too old for a first baby but old enough to have developed
the uterine fibroid tumours in the muscle layer of the
uterine wall which had clouded the safety of this pregnancy from the beginning.

Unfortunately, the fibroids had been small enough to
have sent out no warning signals before she'd conceived.
If he'd known about them before the McNichols had
started trying for a baby, Pete would have recommended
surgery—the procedure was called a myomectomy—
which would in all likelihood have cleared the way for
a normal, healthy pregnancy.

As soon as Patsy had conceived, however, it had been
too late. Pregnancy produced hormones—high levels of
oestrogen and progesterone which stimulated rapid
growth of the fibroids. With the relative positions of the
fibroids and the placenta that he'd seen on more than
one ultrasound scan over the past three months, Mrs
McNichol had been lucky to have had so few problems
thus far.

There'd been signs on the most recent ultrasound,
however, that the baby was no longer getting its opti-
mum amount of nourishment. Although, thanks to the
growth of the fibroids, the uterus itself was now very
large, the baby wasn't.

Patsy was desperate to keep the pregnancy going in
safety. She'd given up work around the family farm
months earlier than she and her husband had originally
planned, and had gone on bed rest as soon as Pete had
mentioned the idea. She'd had two or three episodes of
moderate bleeding which they'd managed to control
through medication, but now there was cramping as well.

A few months from now, when the uterus had returned
to its pre-pregnancy size and her hormone levels had

dropped, Patsy would go under the knife again, so that the fibroids could be safely removed. A future pregnancy would almost certainly be a much safer proposition for her.

First things first, however. Pete was concerned about the extent of the bleeding, and about the ongoing health of an undernourished baby at thirty-three and a half weeks gestation.

If labour could be stopped or slowed, should he send Patsy to Sydney or Canberra? At thirty-three and a half weeks, the baby's required level of care fell just days short of the scope of Glenfallon Hospital's small level two special care facilities. On paper, a few days wasn't much, but how significant was the compromised environment of the uterus?

The clock on the dashboard of his car read six forty-one when he pulled into a reserved space outside the two-storey building which housed Glenfallon Hospital's maternity unit, including its special care facilities and an obstetric operating theatre opened just this year.

The hospital buildings in current use were all relatively new. They were pleasant but rather bland concrete and glass constructions dating from various times over the past twenty-five years when the town had been endowed with capital funds for expansion.

The original building, of gracious old stone with wide verandas, a slate roof and thick walls, was now used for outpatient clinics and support services. The change had been necessary. Apart from its inadequate size, you just couldn't make the old building's layout and facilities accommodate modern medical equipment and practice. Still, stubbornly, Pete liked the old building best. It was the same way he felt about Emma Burns's cottage versus his own newly purchased dwelling.

The new place had a locked double garage with re-mote-controlled doors. It had two bathrooms, and a fam-ily room adjoining the state-of-the-art kitchen. It had a back yard that was currently a depressing expanse of arid soil and builders' rubble but would eventually be a great place for the girls to play whenever they were in resi-dence. He had a landscaping firm scheduled to start work on paths and retaining walls soon.

As with the new hospital buildings, however, he wasn't convinced the house would ever have the right character.

Arriving in the unit, he discovered that, despite their head start, Patsy and Brian McNichol had got there just a few minutes earlier. The departing staff, Kit McConnell and Julie Wong, were both helping the new and nervous patient into a gown and checking her his-tory. She was the delivery ward's only patient at the moment, but the phone was ringing, heralding the pos-sible arrival of someone else.

'How are you feeling, Patsy?' Pete asked at once.

'The contractions are getting stronger. There's one coming now…'

From Patsy's reaction, the pain was quite intense. She couldn't move or speak during its peak, and had to press a thick pad between her legs to deal with the blood. Pete wasn't happy about how much was still flowing. He abandoned any thought of getting her moved to Canberra or Sydney.

This didn't mean he was relaxed about the idea of delivering her here. They could be in for some problems after the birth, and dealing with a post-partum haemor-rhage could be a nightmare. Thank goodness there were a couple of good doctors he could call on.

'Let's get you on your left side with your feet up on

a pillow,' he told his patient, masking the extent of his concern.

She looked pale and drawn. Tired, as if she hadn't been sleeping well in weeks, which was probably the case. Bed rest wasn't fun. No physical activity to promote a healthy fatigue at the end of the day, too much time to think and worry. And she was huge, the size due to her fibroids, not the baby.

Pete palpated the uterus, gave her an internal examination and found that the cervix was ripe, already fully effaced and dilated to six centimetres. The baby's position wasn't good. Feet and bottom down low, and head lying next to her mother's heart. The heartbeat was fine, no sign of distress, and that was a plus. But he really didn't like the bleeding, or his rough impression of the baby's size. He'd been monitoring this for several weeks, and there'd been steady growth, but the baby was still smaller than it should be for this stage of pregnancy.

'I'll be back in a minute,' he promised Patsy, when he'd finished.

Heading for the phone at the nurses' station, he almost cannoned into Emma Burns, who had just arrived, and whom he hadn't seen in the three months he'd been renting her house. She was like a breath of cool, fresh air, scented with spring. She was like her home—bright and pretty and calming.

They smiled at each other.

'Hi,' he said. 'Welcome back.'

'Thanks.'

A beat of uncomfortable silence hung in the air, and neither of them knew what to say. Pete felt there ought to be something better than what he'd come out with thus far. Something witty or meaningful. Something a little private and personal that encompassed all the complex flavours of the e-mails they'd exchanged.

As if he had time to think about it now!

She'd done something to herself while she'd been away, he noted vaguely. Something good. Hair was different. Eyes. Lips. How she'd done it, he didn't know. He didn't even know quite *what* she'd done, he only knew that it was good.

Straight, dark, glossy tresses, arched brows, glowing brown eyes, soft, happy mouth. And yet he didn't even have time to say, Wow! You look great, Emma! Although he definitely wanted to.

'Can you make sure the ob. theatre is fired up and ready to go?' he said. 'No one else in there, is there?'

'No, we're quiet.'

'I'm phoning Gian Di Luzio and Nell Cassidy. I've a got a patient in there…' he gestured at Room One with a backward jab of his thumb over his shoulder '…who's making me nervous.'

'Fill me in,' she said. She had a lovely voice, clear and steady. 'I'm not officially on yet, but I'm obviously going to be in on the surgery, right? I think we've got another labouring mum coming in, but Bronwyn's going to handle her.'

'Yes, I want you in Theatre,' he answered. 'And I expect you'll be moving over to Special Care to look after this baby, if we keep her.'

Emma had spent two years in Sydney, a few years ago, acquiring specialised neonatal nursing qualifications, and staffing was usually juggled to enable her to care for any babies who needed extra attention and skills after birth. There were a couple of other well-qualified nurses to share the load as well.

'Might we not keep her?' she asked.

'I hope we can.' He hadn't quite answered her question with the words, but went on to do so in his description of the patient's history.

Emma's appearance might have changed in three months—what was it? Her eyes glowed! But he doubted whether her capabilities had. She'd always been good. A team player and able to handle all the different types of people she had to deal with, from nervous new fathers to overworked GPs. She was level-headed, thorough and adept at anticipating problems. He sketched out what she needed to know, using a barrage of medical shorthand which had her nodding and frowning at once.

'Yes, I see what you mean,' she said. 'I can see why you'd want Dr Di Luzio and Dr Cassidy.'

Gian Di Luzio was Glenfallon's one obstetrician and gynaecologist, and a woman would have to go quite a distance to find another one. Like most parts of rural Australia, Glenfallon was chronically in need of specialists. As a result, there were several GPs in the area who'd obtained extra credentials in various fields to meet demand.

Pete was one of them. He'd returned to Glenfallon at the beginning of the year after two years spent in Sydney, and he was now better qualified than anyone but Gian in delivering babies and dealing with associated areas, but he was by no means too proud to reach out and grab a fully fledged specialist's extra experience when he needed it. With the twin risks of post-partum haemorrhage and a delicate baby, this was one of those times.

Nell Cassidy was no slouch when it came to extra experience either. She ran the hospital's accident and emergency department with an iron hand, and no velvet gloves involved. She also oversaw the hospital's acute-care patients—adults, children and infants. She was extremely bright, unflappable in a crisis and always the very last person to accept that a patient couldn't be saved.

She'd revived one of Pete's patients last year—a four-year-old girl, the same age as his daughters now were—after a near-drowning, and she'd kept vigilant when everyone else had been ready to celebrate and relax.

Two days after the incident in the back-yard pool, when Amber Szabo had already started smiling and talking and her parents and hospital staff were talking about her discharge, Dr Cassidy had headed off a major organ shutdown, battled death once again and saved the child.

Now, as far as Pete was concerned, the A and E staff could saddle the woman with any unflattering nickname they liked, but he would defend her with spirit all the way.

They had a full team assembled by seven-twenty. They had type A-positive blood waiting for Patsy, and a neonatal resus trolley equipped and waiting for her baby. They had oxygen and intubation equipment, monitors for heart rate, respiratory rate and blood oxygen saturation, and a barrage of drugs on hand.

They had overhead lights switched on, trays of shiny, sterile equipment lined up, and their patient ready to be wheeled in. The pace had picked up in Labour and Delivery, too. The recently delivered mum had been moved across to the post-partum ward, but they had a new admission to take her place—a young woman of nineteen, who'd had only sporadic prenatal care and no second-trimester sonogram, and was uncertain of her dates. Around eight, eight and a half months gone, she thought.

Thirty-six   or   thirty-seven   weeks?   Apparently

Bronwyn Jackson wasn't convinced of this after a manual examination.

'She feels too small,' the midwife reported to Pete. 'By the height of the fundus, I'd say thirty-five weeks, maybe even thirty-four.'

'Can we try to stop the labour?' Pete asked.

'No chance. Fully effaced, half-dilated, contractions every few minutes. This baby's coming today, and we've got the resus trolley on hand.'

'I'll get there for the delivery if I can.'

'The joint is jumping all of a sudden.'

'Better phone Alison Cairns and tell her she might be needed, too.' Dr Cairns was good with fragile babies.

The new admission, Rebecca Childer, had been put down as Pete's patient, although her family was fairly new to Glenfallon, and he'd only ever seen her mother, Susan, for a couple of routine things. He didn't like having this new, questionable labour hanging over his head when Patsy and her baby were uppermost in his mind.

The baby obviously didn't want to stay in Patsy's tumour-filled uterus any longer. He only hoped the little girl would be safe out of there, and in their hands. Should he have sent Patsy to a bigger facility before this? She'd argued against the idea very strongly, but he could have presented it in starker terms.

If we lose this baby, came the insistent thought, how much will I question my own decisions? And where's Rebecca Childer going to be up to in her labour when I get out of Theatre?

'Dr Croft looks terrible,' Emma said quietly to Nell Cassidy.

Although Emma was over a year younger than the A and E specialist, she and Nell had been friends since their school days. More specifically, since the Glenfallon Ladies' College Senior A netball team's memorable trip to Sydney about seventeen years ago, for a round of competitions.

Teenage giggles and confessions during the long bus ride had gradually evolved into the more considered honesty and support of adult friendship, and had survived divergent career paths and life experiences, long periods of living in different places and even some significant criticisms of each other's choices.

Nell knew that Emma considered her too cool and too uncompromising in her approach to her work. Emma knew that Nell would have 'thrown that parasitical stepmother of yours out months ago', instead of putting up with the situation until Beryl had left in a huff to go and live with her own daughter earlier that year.

Somehow, however, these differences of opinion didn't matter. This same honesty now made it possible for the two of them to have a serious, if snatched conversation on an unrelated subject while they waited for their own role in safeguarding the McNichol baby's first minutes of life.

'Terrible is a bit harsh,' Nell said in response to Emma's comment. 'He looks tired, definitely. And stressed.'

'That's what I meant, Nell. It was sympathetic. I wasn't accusing him of having a bad hair day and tacky clothes. *Is* he tired and stressed?'

'Most people are when their marriage is in the process of doing a slow-motion shatter.'

'I thought his marriage was over. In his e-mails, he always… Well, in his e-mails, he sounded better than he looks.'

'These things take time, Emma. But I expect if he's

been talking about his divorce in his e-mails, you know a lot more about it than I do.'

'I know hardly anything,' Emma said quickly.

She was sorry she'd made the initial comment to Nell now. She hadn't meant this to turn into an analysis or a catechism. Having thought of Pete Croft as a kind of penfriend for the past three months, she'd been concerned to see the evidence of stress and problems in his face—problems he'd mentioned to her only in the most oblique way.

Something changed in him when they began the surgery, however. She saw him blink and work the muscles in his face, as if trying to wake them up, and there was a new alertness in his expression, a determination and focus that stripped away the signs of weariness and emotional preoccupation she'd first seen.

Pete was a good-looking man. Somehow, she'd never seen it before. Maybe because he didn't fit the tall-dark-and-handsome model that most women wanted. He was tall enough, yes, but he wasn't a giant—just under six feet, nicely built in an athletic way. He wasn't dark. He did have brown eyes, but they weren't for drowning in. They were too focused, too intelligent, too ready to be amused and too casually kind.

His skin was typically Australian—fair, a little roughened by the power of the sun, and uneven in tone. On a woman, it would have been disastrous skin, but on a man it was…very male. Rugged and strong and casually attractive.

As Nell had pointed out, he hadn't been near a razor that morning, and his beard was growing in fast, a red-gold sheen of stubble surrounding firm lips which looked thin when he was absorbed in his work and fuller when he smiled his generous smile.

His hair was cut so you could see that it started as a very dark, rusty gold and went blonder as it grew out, until it settled on sand mixed with straw as its definitive colour. He had little creases at the corners of his eyelids—creases he needed a woman to kiss away with soft, tender lips—and he had a tanned curve of neck at the back which could make that same woman want to stroke it with her fingers, then thread them upwards into the soft prickle of his hair as she sighed against him.

Only not me, Emma thought in sudden panic. *Why on earth am I suddenly thinking this way?*

'We're good to go here, Houston,' said anaesthetist Harry Ang.

'One day I am going to kill that man,' Nell muttered.

It was one of Dr Ang's harmless quirks that he liked to speak as if this was NASA Mission Control and he was an astronaut about to launch into space. Nell had a limited tolerance for harmless quirks.

Emma didn't mind Dr Ang—he was a nice guy, and always pleasant to the nurses, which counted for a lot—but she had to suppress a laugh all the same when Pete said, 'Apollo Thirteen, do you mind if we cut satellite communications for the rest of this mission?'

'Just trying to raise team morale.'

'Consider it already more than sufficiently raised, Dr Ang,' Nell came in. Her tone could have lasered through glass.

Gian Di Luzio ignored the whole thing. He simply asked for a piece of equipment, and the surgery began. Emma and Nell were standing by, waiting for the baby, and Emma found that her focus stayed fixed on Pete. She'd never realised it would feel so intimate to know that he'd lived in her house, and she wondered if he felt in any way the same.

The intimacy had to be even greater, perhaps. He'd slept in her bed. He'd used her dishes. He'd sat on her couch. Her personal possessions had all been packed away, but rooms were personal, too. Air was personal. Grass was personal. He'd breathed her air and trodden her grass.

He had mowed it very neatly, too, just before he'd left. He'd dumped the fresh clippings from the mower in their usual spot beside the compost bin behind her shed, and she'd arrived home to find them still giving off their tangy, summery smell. It had seemed as if Pete must have left just minutes before.

Pete made the incision in Patsy's abdomen and cut through the outer layers of fat and muscle to reach the uterus. He and Gian had decided on the more conservative midline incision, given the difficult placement of placenta, fibroids and baby.

Gian muttered a couple of suggestions, and Nell stepped close when it was time to lift the baby free. Dr Di Luzio was another very capable doctor, Emma knew, and he'd just become engaged to her fellow midwife and friend, Kit McConnell. The couple were still talking about dates for their wedding, and they'd just agreed to formally adopt his brother's little girl, Bonnie.

'Here we go,' the obstetrician said.

He brought out a blue, slippery bundle of limbs and a tight, immobile little face, beyond the sea of green surgical fabric, and gave the baby girl at once to Nell. Above his mask, Pete looked tense, and the sound they were all waiting for—a baby's cry—hadn't happened yet. The lights were bright on Mrs McNichol's exposed skin, with its rust-coloured splashes of antiseptic, and the seconds seemed to drag.

'She's small for dates. Tiny!' Dr Ang exclaimed.

'We knew she would be,' Pete said, his tone clipped. Nell suctioned the baby's nose and throat out carefully and chafed her chest, but nothing happened. 'Hoping for better than this, though,' Pete added.

'Come on, sweetheart!' Nell muttered. 'Don't scare us like this!'

Working closely beside Nell, Emma clamped and cut the cord. The baby was still limp. Her one-minute Apgar score wouldn't be all that great. Emma calculated automatically. One for tone, one for colour, zero for respiration...

'OK, she's still not breathing. I'm going to bag her, I'm not going to wait,' Nell said, grabbing the equipment quickly.

She laid the baby in the open tray of the resus trolley beneath the warming lights. Emma managed to slip a stretchy little cap on the baby's head to keep vital body heat in. The umbilical stump was the most favoured site for IV insertion in a premmie, but sometimes one needed intravenous lines put in through the veins in its scalp.

She hoped she wouldn't be taking the little hat off again soon for that purpose. A baby at thirty-three weeks shouldn't need that level of treatment. That fibroid-crowded uterus hadn't been good for her at all.

'Got some bleeding here,' Dr Di Luzio said. 'Pete, the placenta's looking very tricky, right across a mass of intramurals. Surprised she got this far with the pregnancy. Not a bit surprised about the size of the baby. Nell?'

'Going as fast as I can here,' she answered. She held the manual oxygen bag to the baby's face, trying to pump air into the tiny lungs and listen with a stethoscope at the same time. Nothing was happening.

'One more try, then I'm going to intubate,' she announced. 'Heart rate's a little slow and thready, and there's a bit of a murmur. It may clear up on its own. They often do. Still, we have to get moving on this.'

Already, nearly two minutes had passed since the clamping of the cord, and every second without oxygen was critical. Thank goodness Patsy was unaware of all this!

'Emma?' Nell prompted.

'Yes.' She had the intubation equipment ready, and the oxygen.

The tube was pitifully small, and it would be an extremely delicate procedure, with the risk of tubing into the stomach instead, creating yet another delay. Nell had her naturally pale face set like a mask as she made her final attempt to squeeze oxygen into the baby's lungs manually.

'Come on, darling,' she repeated, tapping the tiny feet, chafing the chest, looking for the right stimulation.

Normally, her skin complemented her dark blonde hair, but that was all tucked beneath her royal blue disposable cap. She looked as efficient and as cool as a machine, but Emma knew she had a strong, passionate heart beating away underneath.

'OK, we've got her,' Nell announced at last. 'No tube, thank goodness. She's breathing on her own. Yes.' She watched and listened. 'Yes! Heart rate is better already. Colour's improving. She's picking up quickly now.'

The five-minute Apgar score was the crucial one as a predictor of long-term health and development. Emma added the figures again. One for tone, one for colour, two for respiration…Seven. Eight would have been nice, but if she'd added that extra point, she would have been cheating.

'Good. Go for it. Got our own problems over here,' Gian said, in answer to Nell.

'Houston, we have a—' Dr Ang began.

'Shut the hell up, Harry,' Pete sang at him.

'Sure. Sure.'

'Can we tie off this vessel?' the obstetrician asked.

'Got it,' Pete murmured. 'How's the placenta looking?'

Emma didn't have time to look over at the table to see what was happening. She heard Pete's voice, muttering something else, and Dr Ang confirming that everything looked fine at his end, although the patient's blood pressure was beginning to drop.

'OK, placenta's coming away,' Gian said. 'Most of it. Getting a big bleed now.' His voice was calm, almost lazy, but no one was fooled. 'Cautery, Mary Ellen. Good. Thanks. Let's get this closed off.'

There was a hiss, and the acrid smell of burning.

'Good *girl*, what a lovely pink colour now! What great breathing!' Nell said, as if it was the baby's own success, not hers, and perhaps she was right. She leaned closer, listened once more just to check. 'You good, darling girl! *Now* we've got it all happening,' she crooned at the tiny baby, still working quickly as she spoke.

She taped a pulse oximeter to the baby's hand, checked the fluctuating numbers that appeared on the screen. Climbing. Pink had now begun to radiate outwards from torso to extremities. Emma blinked back tears of relief. Blue was just the wrong colour for a baby, frightening and wrong. Pink was like the sun coming out on a cold, cloudy day, lifting spirits at once.

'Thank God!' she whispered.

She saw Pete's glance cut across in her direction from the table. His face looked frozen for a moment, stark.

He was thirty-six, she knew, but he looked forty today. A very masculine, competent, good-looking but stressed-out forty. Her fingers suddenly itched to smooth the lines on his face, to trace the shape of his mouth until it softened beneath her touch.

Then he blinked those tired brown eyes with their creased lids, grinned at her and nodded, wordlessly sharing her prayer of relief. She grinned back, and felt a rush of warmth and happiness. Gian's running commentary suggested he had the bleeding in hand. Most importantly, the baby girl was breathing.

Emma wasn't, as she smiled at Pete.

She seemed to be floating a good three inches above the ground, and she wasn't breathing at all.

But at the moment breathing didn't seem remotely important.

CHAPTER TWO

'DR CROFT, we've got Rebecca in transition and almost ready to push,' said Bronwyn. She was an efficient, thin and rather cool brunette, married with a school-aged son and daughter.

'Right.'

Pete took a deep breath, switched his focus quickly. Little Lucy McNichol was looking good now, better than he'd dared to hope. She was small, just over three pounds on the old scale, but after that initial, frightening hitch with her breathing, she seemed reasonably strong, and she'd even taken the breast.

Nell had said she thought the gestational age might be closer to thirty-five or thirty-six weeks, not the thirty-three he'd been working on. Patsy might have mistaken bleeding at the beginning of the pregnancy for a period, and he'd dated the baby on that basis. With the spread and position of the fibroids retarding growth, the ultrasound scan at seventeen weeks hadn't contradicted those dates.

But now here was Rebecca Childer about to give birth, and Bronwyn thought her dates might be wrong in the other direction. With no accurate date of LMP—last menstrual period—and no ultrasound measurements, they were working purely on the measurement from pelvic bone to top of uterus.

'Don't be surprised if you get called back up here,' he told Nell, as she stripped off gloves and mask and prepared to head back down to A and E. 'We have another iffy pregnancy on hand.'

'I'll be back up here anyway as soon as I can, just to make sure Lucy's doing as well as we think,' she said. 'I did hear a faint murmur over her heart, did I tell you? But, of course, that's very common. I'll let it go as long as her stats are good.'

'It's your call. She looked good to me, too.'

'See you in a while.' Nell went towards the lift.

'Rebecca, how are you doing here?' Pete asked his new patient, as he entered Delivery Room Two.

She didn't answer, just gave him a hostile look which he shrugged off. If he hadn't asked about her state, the look would have been just as grim. In the grip of a powerful contraction, she wasn't enjoying herself at the moment.

As soon as the contraction was over, he gave her a manual exam. It wasn't routine policy to do so in this department, but Rebecca wanted a progress report. He listened to the baby. Heartbeat was fine. Dilatation was almost complete. The head was nice and low, but small. He agreed with Bronwyn. This wasn't a thirty-seven-weeker.

'Have we got extra staff?' he muttered to her.

'Vanessa Gunn is coming in,' Bronwyn answered. 'Emma will go into Special Care, with back-up from Sue North in post-partum. We'll juggle it.'

Rebecca moaned. 'I'm not ready for this. Nobody said it would be this bad.'

'You're doing really well, Rebecca,' Bronwyn told her.

'Don't give me that garbage…'

Pete listened to the heart again, and found that the

rate was perceptibly slower. 'Get Dr Cassidy up here again,' he told Bronwyn. 'We might not need her, but if we do, I don't want to wait.'

'What about Emma?'

'Her, too, as long as the post-partum staff have got Lucy's care covered.'

Rebecca groaned, half sat up and opened her legs. The head was already crowning, propelled forward by the action of the uterus. Contractions were coming without a pause in between. Rebecca strained again. They'd have a baby very soon...

'OK,' Nell said. 'She's stable. She's good.'

Like Patsy, Rebecca had delivered a tiny girl, whom she'd named Alethea. It was an old-fashioned name, but it was pretty, Emma thought. She clung to this thought— that the baby's name was pretty, that the baby was pretty—because the little creature had problems at the moment.

She'd needed intubation and she was on a respirator. It had taken Nell, Emma and Pete an hour to get her stabilised enough to move her to Special Care, and Nell, who'd actually thought that was 'nice and fast' under the circumstances, was still working over her with a severe frown on her face.

Pete had left to check on Patsy McNichol.

'Oxygen saturation's gone up,' Nell said. 'I like her heart rate. I like how quickly we got this done. I like most things.'

'That's good.'

'For the moment. And I'm hoping we'll get her off the respirator within the next couple of days.'

'What's worrying you, Nell?' Emma said. She knew her friend well enough to realise there was something.

'I don't know.' She shook her head, as if to clear swimming-pool water from her ears. 'I think I'm hearing a murmur again.'

'Lucy had one, too.'

'I know. They're so common in babies, especially early babies, and mostly they mean nothing. With Lucy, I wasn't so concerned. Her dates were better, even though she was almost as small. A small baby delivered within a few weeks of term is almost always better off than a larger one delivered earlier.'

'And this one wasn't large, in any case.'

'I know. Which worries me, too, because I don't know why.' Nell listened to the heartbeat again. 'I don't know whether to be concerned about this baby's murmur either,' she said. 'Certainly want to get the rest of her stronger before we start worrying about her heart. Hey, Alethea? Do you support that plan, darling? You don't want a whole lot more mucking around, do you?'

Her voice was soft and cooing as she addressed the motionless baby. Then she straightened and spoke to Emma again.

'All indications are that the heart is working fine at the moment,' she said. 'If it wasn't, her numbers wouldn't look so good. If I keep hearing this, though, or if it changes, I'm going to do a couple of tests. Let me know if there are any indications that her heart isn't doing its job.'

'She's premature…' Emma said.

'I'm guessing thirty-three or thirty-four weeks.'

'So… Patent ductus arteriosus is a fairly common condition in premmies, isn't it? Treatable, too.'

Emma knew that in a normal foetal heart, the ductus arteriosus was open. In a full-term baby, this vessel closed automatically at birth, as part of the heart's almost miraculous shift from foetal circulation to the circulation pattern it sustains throughout its life. A premmie baby's heart can't always manage this shift on its own, however, and if the ductus remains open beyond early infancy, permanent heart damage could result. Fortunately, the condition could be monitored and treated if necessary.

'If it's that, and if the PDA doesn't close on its own, there's a drug we can use to encourage it,' Nell agreed. 'It doesn't always work, and that'll mean surgery.'

'In Sydney.'

'A few years ago, we'd have had no hope of handling a baby like this in Glenfallon at all, with or without the need for surgery. Even now, I wonder if we should be starting to look at arranging medivac transport.'

'We're a level two unit.' Emma was a little defensive. 'I've handled several thirty-four-weekers, and even a couple of younger ones whose mothers had their dates wrong, like this one did.'

'Yes, I'm not kicking her out of here yet, am I, Alethea? There are no real danger signs, and it would be great if we could get her strong and well ourselves…but I still think Sydney's on the cards.'

'There's no point in having the facilities to handle premmies here if we don't use them to maximum potential,' Emma said. 'Thirty-four weeks is the cut-off, I know, but personally I'm trained to a higher level than that.'

'True. And people get better at it if they practise. There are going to be a few of us practising on this baby.'

'Don't put it like that, Nell, as if she's an anatomical model.'

'Oh, I'm not. I'm not. You know I'm not. I'm just

nervous. That thumb-pricking feeling that something's not right, despite all the things that clearly are.'

'The way you were worried about that little girl who was revived after she fell in her pool?'

'She was Pete's patient, too.'

'This one was dropped into his lap,' Emma pointed out, although why she felt this instinct to leap to Pete's defence, she didn't know. 'He'd never seen her before.'

'The man has trouble with the women in his life, doesn't he?' Nell commented lightly. 'Whether they're patients or family.'

Emma bit back a comment which she might regret. Was Nell implying Pete's troubles were his fault? Again, she felt a need to protect him and to leap to his defence, which she didn't understand. He was extremely competent and very intelligent. He worked hard, he cared and he had the right priorities. Just because he'd been living in her house, that didn't mean he needed her nurturing. What was wrong with her today?

'Let's take this one across to the unit,' Nell added.

It took them another hour to get the baby settled in Glenfallon's tiny special care unit, which was simply a small, closed-off room with thick, almost soundproof windows opening onto the rest of the maternity unit. It was most often staffed by the midwives rostered for post-partum care.

Lucy was already there, in the care of Sue North now, but she'd probably go home with her mother in a few days' time, if her condition continued to be this good and she began to feed properly. Alethea's arrival would necessitate the juggling of staff so that Emma and a roster of two or three other experienced nurses could provide her with the acute care she'd need at first, round the clock.

In the meantime, Nell was staying.

'I hope my department's quiet,' she said. 'No doubt I'll hear the yelling soon enough if it isn't! We can let the dad come in and see Lucy now.'

Brian McNichol had been shepherded aside as soon as Patsy had been taken into the operating theatre. He'd probably been fed several gallons of tea by now. Emma had lost track of time. Where was Patsy? Still in Recovery? After her general anaesthesia and the extent of her bleeding, she'd probably be kept there for longer than usual. Had her husband been able to see her yet?

'I'll track him down,' she said.

'Rebecca Childer, too. She might need some encouragement. She seemed a little frightened about what to expect, and inclined to suggest it was all up to the nurses. Or her mother!'

'We'll work on that. I'll hunt up some pamphlets on premmies, and talk to her and her mother as well, try and get her involved right from the beginning.'

Emma went back to the nurses' station on the labour and delivery side of the unit, and found an unnatural level of quiet. No patients.

'Just had a phone call from a first-timer in query early labour, but it sounded to me like a false alarm,' Bronwyn summarised, lifting her head from the paperwork she was catching up on. 'She's not due for a couple of weeks. She wants to come in, but I expect we'll be sending her home again. Pete Croft is chugging coffee in the kitchen if you want a progress report on Mrs McNichol.'

'Oh, I do!' Emma said. 'And I'm hunting for the dad.'

'I sent him off for breakfast. He was wandering around like a ghost.'

'Dr Cassidy says Rebecca can see her baby now. Have you moved her to her room?'

'Yes, half an hour ago,' Bronwyn answered. 'And her mother's with her. I'll take Brian McNichol round to Special Care as soon as he gets back from breakfast.'

As Bronwyn had said, Emma found Pete in the kitchen.

He'd evidently 'chugged' his coffee to good effect, and was holding his mug beneath the wall-mounted urn to fill it for a second time—or possibly a third—when Emma entered the room. He took a gulp of it black, then shuddered, grabbed the milk carton and splashed in a generous amount, before bringing the mug to his lips again.

Only then did he turn and see her standing there, and she had to quickly hide the awareness she suspected had been showing in her face. 'Emma...' he said, coming back to the present from what looked like a million miles away.

'I was wondering...Mrs McNichol?' she asked, before the beat of awkwardness could lengthen.

'She lost a lot of blood,' Pete answered. 'Not enough to need a transfusion, but she's on a fast drip and I'll be watching her iron levels over the next few months. Thank goodness the baby started breathing when she did!'

'What's your sense about Alethea Childer?' Emma asked.

'I wanted to ask you that, actually, since you've been with her all the way through. How much did she weigh?'

'Twelve-fifty grams.'

'And we estimated thirty-three weeks gestation!' He pressed his lips together, and she couldn't help watching as they softened again when he continued to speak. 'That's small, even for the dates.'

'I know.' An average baby should have weighed several hundred grams more. 'And Dr Cassidy doesn't know why.'

'Bothering her?'

'Yes. She picked up a heart murmur as well, which she's not sure about yet.'

'Lucy McNichol has one, too.'

'This time she thinks it may be more significant, but so far the heart is doing the job with no problems, so we're hanging fire.'

'Right.' Pete shut his eyes for a moment, then opened them again. A tiny muscle twitched just above one cheekbone. 'I guess I'm not all that surprised. Has the staffing been sorted?'

Emma nodded. 'Yes, looks like it. Sue North knows what she's doing. I'm in there, too, and they'll juggled the roster. We're all used to stretching when we have to.'

'It may not be for long, if we end up sending Alethea Childer somewhere else.'

'You don't want to?'

'Funny, but, no, I don't.' He gave an upside-down smile. His eyes had those creases around them again. 'You'd think I might be keen to get this one off my hands. But she dropped on us out of the blue, and for some reason I don't want to lose her again to another hospital just as quickly. Rebecca's young. She has no confidence, and she's not ready for this.'

'She seems a little detached at this stage, like she might leave everything to us and just stay away.'

'Maybe that explains why I'm feeling possessive.'

He leaned back against the kitchen countertop, with one elbow resting on it. The movement made his shirt tighten across his strong chest. The fluorescent light overhead sculpted shadows on the side of his face.

'I feel like the baby belongs here,' he went on. 'And that we can do what we need to for her, with Nell on board. Unless that heart murmur turns out to be significant and she needs surgery. That, we couldn't handle. That would mean Sydney or Melbourne.'

He took another gulp of his coffee, punctuating the heaviness of the statement. The movement firmed his mouth and stretched the planes of his cheeks a little.

'If it's an open ductus, the operation itself isn't that complex any more, is it?' Emma asked.

'In relative terms, I guess. It's a closed-heart procedure.'

'They don't have to open the heart itself.' Emma understood this.

'And no heart-lung machine required,' Pete confirmed. 'Start to finish, less than an hour. They make an opening in the left side of her chest, tie off the PDA and divide it. It's about the width of a piece of string.'

'Oh, huge!' she drawled.

'As I said, simple is relative. It would still need to be done in a major children's hospital, by a paediatric surgeon. And what parent wants to think of a baby as small as Alethea in surgery when she's just a few days old, no matter how skilled those guys are?'

'I know.' Emma leaned against the fridge and rubbed an aching calf with the side of her shoe. 'Nell has hopes the murmur doesn't mean anything. The baby's oxygen saturation is up in the high nineties.'

'That's great! Are you heading back to Special Care now?' He tipped out the rest of his coffee, rinsed the mug and rested it upside down on the sink.

'Yes, I just wanted to catch up with you and make sure everything was still in hand on this side of the unit.'

'Come on, then,' he said.

He slipped past her and she followed in his wake at once. They walked along the U-shaped corridor together in a comfortable silence, and found Nell scribbling notes on Alethea's chart, while Lucy slept peacefully. Both babies looked like tiny red frogs in the white expanse of their special, warmed humidicribs.

'I'm heading off,' Nell said, capping her pen. 'I'll be back in a couple of hours. Or sooner if you need me, Emma. If that oxygen sat rate drops, if the heart rate changes, you know what I'm looking for. Pete, she's not as strong as you hoped. And there may—*may*—be a heart problem.'

'Yes.' He nodded. 'Emma told me. You're going to wait before doing any tests?'

'Yes, as long as her levels are this good, but I want to talk to the mother about whether to send her to a higher level unit even if she doesn't need surgery. There may be other problems. I just have that feeling, despite what the machines are saying. And this is a stretch for us.'

'I know, Nell, but if there's nothing specific, and if the mother is already too detached to get properly—'

'Look, I'm not saying it's an easy decision,' she cut in. 'There are pros and cons.'

'There are always those.'

She ignored him. 'We have to consider the downside of transporting a fragile baby, for a start. And you're right. Taking a premmie away from a mother whose bonding is already tenuous could cause its own problems. But let's think about it,' she urged, her eyes bright. 'Let's get it right.'

She left without giving him time to reply, and Emma saw his jaw set.

Anger, or determination?

She wasn't sure.

She didn't think Pete was the kind of doctor who'd make up his mind and then stick to his guns out of ego and pride. She'd only ever seen him put the interests of his patients first. But she knew he was under pressure at the moment in his personal life, and there were pulls in both directions for Alethea.

Pete looked again at the baby and at the fluctuating red figures on the monitor, and Emma couldn't help doing the same. The heart rate, respiration and oxygen saturation all showed up on screen at a glance. The baby's nappy was as small and flat as an envelope. The little hat covered the whole of her tiny head, and her face looked as crumpled and ancient and inscrutable as that of an Eastern mystic.

'Should we start trying for a bed in Sydney or Melbourne straight away?' Pete muttered. He might have been talking to himself. 'On paper, we've got the facilities and the staff. I'm glad I called in Nell.'

'She's good,' Emma agreed.

So was he. Thorough and caring and imaginative in his approach. He wasn't afraid to try something new, or to go out on a limb.

He was way out on a precarious one right at this moment, putting Rebecca's chance to bond with her baby on a par with the baby's potential need for a higher level of care. On the other hand, skin-to-skin human contact had been shown in repeated studies to be as physically important to a premmie's development as oxygen, medication and specialist expertise.

He looked up.

'Sorry. I'm still e-mailing you. Only verbally this time.' He grinned, and there was a warm glint in his brown eyes that she responded to at once with a laugh.

'Are you?'

'That doesn't make sense,' he conceded. 'But it was nice, Emma. Did I say that?'

'You said it was a slice of paradise. My house. In your card, I mean.' Emma cleared her throat. 'You didn't specifically mention the e-mails.'

She felt absurdly self-conscious beneath the warm wash of his words. In the confined space, they were standing closer than she felt comfortable with. It was ridiculous to be so aware of him, to feel this sense of closeness and this sense of knowing him, which was based on such a thin foundation.

'Well, the e-mails were good,' he said. 'They helped.'

Emma blurted, 'Is it Claire? Is that why you're looking so stressed?' Then could have cut out her tongue. He'd said nothing to encourage her to ask such a personal question. It was all coming from her.

He sighed, then muttered, 'Yes, of course it's Claire.'

'I'm sorry, you don't have to—'

'I thought that we were in the home stretch.' His mouth tightened and turned down. He spoke in a low, rapid way, and didn't look at her. 'We had decisions made and arrangements worked out. I thought. But Claire's thrown that to the four winds, and I would have done so even if she hadn't, because of the way she's been behaving. I don't know what's wrong with her.'

He stopped, and looked up suddenly, with a ravaged expression that struck Emma to the heart. She felt the same need to touch him that had tingled in her fingers before. The same need to smooth out those creases around his eyes and softly stroke the brown skin at the back of his neck, to press his lips with her fingertips until they relaxed, and to tell him everything would be all right.

'Oh, Pete!' she said. It was heartfelt, but so inadequate.

'I haven't talked to anyone about this.' His eyes were narrowed, and glittered with fatigue. 'I don't know why I'm talking to you.' He gave a short laugh. 'Because you're listening, I guess. Because you asked. You were here at the right moment, basically. The *wrong* moment, perhaps.'

'I shouldn't have asked. I'm sorry.'

'No, it was fine. Only now I'm not offering you much choice about listening to a far more detailed reply than you wanted.'

'I-it's fine, Pete,' she stammered, echoing the same word he'd used—safe and vague. 'I'm happy—that is, I want to listen. If it's a help.'

'I'm petitioning for sole custody. Please, don't talk to anyone about this!'

'As if I would!'

He glanced around to check that the door was closed and that they were fully alone.

'Couldn't find a house I liked as much as yours,' he said quietly. Emma had to step even closer in order to hear him, and came within range of his body heat and his clean male smell. 'I've rushed into it. Had to, because I wanted a home for the girls. It's part of that new development up on the hill overlooking the river.'

'It'll be beautiful when the gardens get going. I've driven through it. There are some lovely places.'

'I know. But right now it's arid. And I shouldn't even begin to mind about that, because it's the least of my problems. I don't know what's wrong with Claire,' he repeated.

'If you need anything, Pete...' Emma offered, while wondering if even this token formula was overstepping the bounds. They *weren't* friends. They were only colleagues, and he'd recently paid her three months of rent. The fact that they were standing this close didn't mean anything personal.

'Might,' he answered. The single word told her nothing about how he'd received her offer. 'I'll let you know.'

'Please, do.'

He nodded briefly, then looked at both babies' monitors again, and she watched him literally turn his back on the brief moments of confession. With his back to her, he cleared his throat, massaged his temples with the thumb and middle finger of one hand, squared his shoulders, then turned to her again. 'Patsy's out of Recovery and in a private room. She wants to see the baby.'

'Mary Ellen can organise that. She's probably with Patsy now, starting to get her mobile.'

'Keep me posted on any change in how Alethea's doing. I want to be as involved as I can.'

'Of course. You and Dr Cassidy are both down as her doctors.'

'I'd better go. For some strange reason, a lot of other people in this town have the idea I'm their doctor as well!' His smile was warm and kindled flame in his brown eyes, but Emma saw the effort in it and it soon faded.

Something vital seemed to leave the atmosphere of the room as soon as he'd gone.

CHAPTER THREE

'AND Dr Cassidy wants to be told the moment there's any change in her numbers or her appearance or—'

'OK, so any change at all, basically,' summarised Jane Cameron, the midwife who was about to take over baby Alethea's care for this shift.

It was already four o'clock, and Emma was late finishing. She still felt reluctant to go, and didn't understand why, until Pete Croft appeared in the doorway.

I was hoping he'd show up again, and I didn't want to leave until I'd seen him, she realised.

'Still here?' he asked vaguely, and she nodded, feeling foolish.

'I'm about to head off,' she said.

'What about the mum? Where's she?'

'She wanted a same-day discharge.'

'You mean she's already gone?'

'Her mother took her home about half an hour ago. There was no medical reason to say no. Unfortunately.'

'Yes, we would have liked to keep her here for the baby's sake.'

'She was feeling good. No temp. Stomach so flat already you'd hardly know she'd given birth.'

'What's the mother like?' he asked. 'Rebecca's mother, I mean. Susan. I've only had her in and out of my office for such trivial things that I barely remember her.'

'She seems very sensible. I gave the instruction sheets about post-partum care to her, not to Rebecca.'

'Rebecca wouldn't read them?'

'Or follow their suggestions if she did, I suspect. Um, Jane, I'm going to head off,' she added to the other midwife.

'Yes, go. You're late already.'

'Let me take a look at her,' Pete said, speaking to Jane. He picked up the baby's notes and glanced through them. 'Dr Cassidy's been here again,' he murmured.

'See you tomorrow,' Emma said to no one in particular, and Pete only glanced up for a second as he muttered an acknowledgement of her words.

Emma and Pete saw too much of each other over the next two days, but all of their contact revolved around the two small newborns in Emma's care, and if there were any small windows for a more personal interlude between them, neither he nor she chose to open those windows up.

Emma was happy to work another long shift on Wednesday, her mood closely tied to baby Alethea's progress, or lack of it. Patsy McNichol was an almost constant presence while her little Lucy remained in the neonatal annexe, but by Thursday morning the baby girl had begun to feed with consistent strength and appetite, and was looking so good that, in the absence of further problems, she would soon be moved to Patsy's room, ready for discharge on Friday.

Rebecca Childer had only been seen in the unit once, very briefly on Wednesday morning, since her same-day discharge on Tuesday afternoon. During her visit, she had to be coaxed to talk to her baby and to touch her. She seemed frightened that allowing herself to love the baby might prove too painful, and she seemed frightened of the baby, too—so fragile and tiny and different from the fat, healthy, pink ones she'd seen on television commercials for disposable nappies and baby food.

Alethea was still in a precarious condition, with her respiration the biggest problem at this stage, despite the fact that she'd now come off the respirator and was on a mask. Her breathing alarm went off regularly, because she would simply forget to breathe. Emma usually just tickled her feet to get her started again, but it was an indication that she was fragile.

Nell had ordered a precise and detailed monitoring of every aspect of the baby's system, including the recording of every millilitre of fluid that went in and out, every nuance of temperature change and oxygen saturation reading.

The heart murmur wasn't clear or conclusive, and Nell was reluctant to perform tests straight away. Not until Alethea was breathing better. Not until her weight had started to claw its way back to what it had been at birth, after the normal initial loss. Not until the drug they'd given her to close that patent ductus had had a chance to work.

The potential need for transport to Sydney or Melbourne remained Nell's greatest concern at this stage, and she'd muttered a couple more times in Emma's hearing, 'Something's not right...and yet the figures suggest she's doing well. Am I borrowing trouble here?'

It was heart-rending to see the difference in size between Alethea and the two healthy babies born in the unit since her own delivery on Tuesday morning. Patsy herself talked about it in poignant terms in relation to her own tiny Lucy.

'To me those other babies look so huge,' she said to Emma on Thursday, just before lunchtime. 'Almost unnatural. Like the offspring of giants. Yet I know that it's my baby who's the wrong size. And she's lost a hundred and fifty grams since she was born. When will she put it back on and start to gain?'

'Soon,' Emma promised, because she was promising herself the same thing about both babies. 'That weight loss is normal. She's feeding, and that's great. She's getting fluid, and she's getting your antibodies for immunity.'

'Will I really be able to take her home with me?'

'We hope so. It's looking that way.'

Patsy was able to hold her baby easily at least. With Alethea, however, the process was far more of an effort, and Emma had to schedule it into her day in order to fit it in. It had to be done with care, given the equipment to which she was still attached. If Rebecca herself had been here, Emma would have had more time.

But apart from that one uncomfortable visit, Rebecca stayed away.

Her mother was the one to come and see Alethea. She seemed to love the baby very much, but was obviously torn.

'My daughter should be doing this. Is my coming in just encouraging her to pretend this isn't happening?' she said to Emma on Thursday afternoon, and Emma didn't really have an answer. She was pleased that the baby had *someone*, and wondered if Mrs Childer would have spent even more time here if she hadn't been so worried about Rebecca's lack of interest.

Nell came up to the unit several times a day, poring over the detailed figures noted on Lucy's and Alethea's charts. Alethea was passing urine, which meant her kidneys and heart were both doing their jobs. Her feeds came via a nasogastric tube, which she occasionally seemed to be fighting. That wasn't a bad sign either. Some babies were too weak to fight the discomfort of the tube. She also had an IV line for medication and fluids.

Pete dropped in on his way to his practice each morning, on the way home each night, and at any other time he happened to be at the hospital, and Emma knew that she counted on his visits more than she should, just as she'd done on Tuesday, when she'd hung around for that extra hour. By Friday afternoon, there was a sense of something hanging in the air, waiting to happen, but she didn't understand where it came from, or what it meant.

It worried her.

Pete dropped the girls off at his sister's at eight-thirty on Saturday morning. He had office appointments, as usual, from nine until one, and then some patients to see at the hospital. Alethea was, of course, at the top of his list. Lucy and her mother were doing fine, and had been discharged as planned the previous morning.

'Thanks, Jackie,' he told his sister, as soon as the girls had run off to play with their older cousins. 'This would be impossible without you.'

'I can't go on doing it forever, though, Pete,' she told him gently, sliding a mug of coffee across the kitchen bench and into his hand. He hadn't asked for it, but didn't turn it down. 'It would be easier if Mum and Dad were able to share the load.'

'I wouldn't ask. I know Mum's fully tied up, dealing with Dad. And I wish...' He stopped and shrugged.

Jackie knew what the end of the unfinished sentence would have been. Their parents had moved to a retirement unit last year, and their father had a weak heart and type II diabetes. Pete would have liked to have spent more time with them, but how did he fit it in? Jackie did her best in that area, and these emergency sessions of looking after his girls weren't easy on her.

'Mum understands,' Jackie said, answering the statement he hadn't made. 'And so do I.'

'I know,' he said. 'You've both been great. Not to sound like a condemned man, but how long have I got before the axe falls?'

'Until you work something out. An arrangement that's going to last, Pete. Is Claire able to...?'

'She went to Canberra yesterday. Some project. She needed to see a government minister.'

'To do with work?'

Claire had a part-time job with a large local winery. It consisted of basic office assistance, and didn't match her qualifications or her skill level, but she'd been hoping for promotion and increased hours. If the company had sent her to Canberra, perhaps that meant she had been given some additional tasks lately.

'I assume so,' Pete answered his sister. 'I don't know.'

'The two of you don't talk much, do you?' she drawled.

'Understatement, Jackie. I'm so angry with her, I can't see straight where she's concerned, and she never explains anything properly. Apparently, several times lately she hasn't turned up to collect the girls from preschool. No phone call, no alternative arrangement made and Claire herself unreachable. The teachers have had to stay on until she showed up, or they've sent the girls home with another parent. Once it was nearly six before Claire bothered to track them down.'

'Goodness!' Jackie clicked her tongue and frowned. 'The teachers didn't try to phone you?'

'Claire had given them various stories about my being

away and unavailable and uninterested. I've set them straight now. What they think of it all, I don't know.'

'Have you *tried* talking to her?'

'Have you tried collecting water in a sieve? We need a consistent, workable arrangement, but Claire won't see that.'

'You've seen Jim Braithwaite, though, haven't you?' Jackie herself had recommended the family law specialist.

'Yes, and he and I have put the custody petition together, but we have to wait for the hearing. In the meantime, the girls are in limbo, and I'm bending over backwards trying to keep them from feeling as uncertain about their future as I do.'

'Have you talked to anyone else about this?'

Pete hesitated, hearing the hole in the conversation like a giant resonance in the air, then answered, 'No.'

What about Emma? He'd talked to her. Sort of. Without planning to. He'd said too much, and not enough, and none of the right things, and she'd listened to him with more focus and care than he'd had any right to expect.

He still had a clear mental picture of her brown-eyed gaze fixed on him with such concern. She hadn't said much in response to his outpouring. Her halting phrases had suggested she probably thought she'd been inadequate.

She hadn't. There was just nothing that anyone could say.

This was his life, his problem. His, and the girls', and Claire's. He even felt uncomfortable about Jackie's well-meant suggestions and sympathetic noises, and he deeply regretted having talked to Emma. Dragging her into it. Sending the wrong message.

It didn't help to have more people knowing about this, more people putting on Jackie's brisk, supportive expression. He should keep as much of this to himself as possible, from now on. He definitely shouldn't have talked to Emma. He'd said it was e-mail, but he'd never e-mailed her with that sort of detail about his problems.

'You have to pin Claire down,' Jackie said.

'There's only one way to do that. Through the family court. I've tried everything else.'

Still, he felt in his bones that there was another kind of crisis building—felt it the way you could sometimes feel a late summer storm building in the air, even before you heard the thunder and saw the clouds.

And if he was right about this vague thing that he couldn't begin to measure or chart, then he needed to stay on top of his emotions, to stay strong, and in control. He needed, too, to steer clear of distractions and involvements. His sudden awareness of Emma Burns as an attractive, desirable woman since her return from Paris was the last thing he wanted, and the last thing that could be of any help to anyone now.

'I talked to the manager of the child care centre yesterday,' he told his sister, pulling his focus back with difficulty. 'They have a couple of part-time staff who'll take on private babysitting. One's coming over this afternoon for a talk about what's involved.'

'That's great!'

'Well, it feels at the moment like I'm adding another piece of scaffolding to a structure that's already in danger of total collapse, but at least it will take the pressure off you.'

'I didn't mean to push, Pete. I'm very willing. It's just that with Mum and Dad, and also for the girls' sake…'

'Believe me, *everything* at the moment is for the girls'

sake,' he said, hearing the grating harshness in his voice. He took one more gulp of coffee and listened to the noises coming from the other room. 'Sounds like they're happy with Tyler and Sarah, so I won't make a big deal out of saying goodbye to them. I'll be back after lunch, probably around two or so.'

Jackie gave him a quick hug and he knew he was rigid in her arms, armoured as if for a battle.

'Have you put on weight, Alethea? You have!' Emma said.

It was a tiny amount. Twenty grams. Less than an ounce on the imperial scale. But it was a good sign, all the same.

'You are a cute girl,' Emma told her.

Rebecca had visited the baby twice now. The second time, yesterday afternoon, she'd come with her mother, who'd urged her, 'Sing to her or something, love.'

'She can't hear, can she?'

'Of course she can!'

But Rebecca had remained tentative, and hadn't yet visited today. Emma felt that she'd better coo to the baby instead, so that Alethea would at least come to know the sound of a caring human voice. It wasn't a hardship for her to do so.

'We are going to get you breathing room air, and get you growing and feeding, and you'll be home in no time,' she said.

Baby Alethea was receiving her mother's expressed breast-milk through the nasogastric tube now, and this was the best possible nourishment for her. Emma suspected there'd been some heavy lobbying from Rebecca's mother to encourage her to breast-feed, and it was Mrs Childer who brought the tiny quantities of expressed breast-milk in to the hospital each day.

Susan Childer had made a couple of oblique references to the fact that Rebecca was having trouble with the pumping process, too, and when Rebecca appeared, at last, just after lunch, looking as hesitant, miserable and fearful as ever, Emma decided to take some action.

'Things are quiet in the unit at the moment, Rebecca,' she said. 'And Alethea's asleep and peaceful. Would you like one of the other nurses to give you some help with the breast pump? Your mum says you're tearing out your hair.'

'It's awful!' the young mother agreed. 'I hate the whole thing! How can anyone help?'

'Well, I know it seems like a pretty weird thing to be an expert in—'

'You got that right!' Rebecca rolled her eyes. '*I* don't want to be!'

'But we do have a couple of midwives on staff who are specially trained in helping new mothers with feeding, including using a pump.'

'I was thinking I'd just ride it out until the milk dries up, and go with bottle-feeding. It's painful! Mum's nagging me to death, though.'

'The nipple soreness doesn't last, although, of course, it's your decision. Letting the milk dry up can be painful, too, for a few days. Would you like to talk to someone at least?'

'OK. I 'spose so.'

Not exactly an enthusiastic response, but enough to allow Emma to dial the desk at the nurses' station and summon Kit McConnell.

'Let's go somewhere quiet, where no one's going to disturb us,' the other midwife told Rebecca, and the

young mother allowed herself to be led away, still looking miserable. She glanced at the baby on her way out,
opened her mouth, then shook her head, as if deciding
there was no point in saying anything to her tiny, sleeping child.

'Let's hope Kit can help your mum to get better at
the pumping stuff, little girl,' Emma told the baby when
Rebecca had gone. 'Because it's the best thing for you,
and we do so want you to grow for us! Oh, yes, we do,
oh, yes we do,' she crooned, bending over the baby's
special bassinet.

Then she straightened, a little embarrassed, to focus
on Pete standing in the doorway. She smiled at him, felt
the heat building in her face and said awkwardly, 'OK,
yes, you caught me out, talking baby talk.' She raised
her hands in mock surrender. 'No point in mounting a
defence. I confess everything!'

But the baby talk wasn't the reason she'd flushed.
That was all about Pete himself. He didn't laugh at her
lame attempt at humour.

'Don't get too attached,' he said.

His voice was stiff and cool, and his gaze clashed with
hers for one violent moment, before sliding away to look
at the figures on Alethea's monitor. He wasn't wearing
a doctor's white coat, but was dressed casually, the way
most doctors dressed in Glenfallon when their schedule
included a mix of office hours, hospital visits and private
time.

He wore twill weave pants in a neutral sandy shade,
rubber-soled leather loafers and a buttoned, long-sleeved
shirt in a low-key abstract pattern. No tie, and there was
a pair of sunglasses jutting out of his breast pocket and
a stethoscope draped around his neck.

The casual dress and the cool, distant manner didn't

quite fit together, but they were both effective. He looked both attractive and forbidding, and the sensations and emotions that coiled inside Emma were far too complex and unwarranted.

'It's always a mistake to get your emotions involved,' he added.

'She's doing really well,' Emma answered obliquely. She ran her hands down the sides of her blue uniform dress, feeling her palms grow damp.

'She's not yours.'

'I know that, Pete.'

You care about her, too, she wanted to tell him. I know you do. So isn't this a little hypocritical?

But it didn't take much diagnostic effort on her part to realise that her feelings about baby Alethea weren't the real issue, and certainly weren't the most important one.

Pete regretted everything he'd said the other day. He'd closed off. He was sending out some pretty clear signals that his problems at home were not her business, and that he didn't want her to trespass into that territory.

Emma understood.

She'd almost been expecting it, which was probably why...partly why...she hadn't tried to talk to him on a personal level since Tuesday.

That didn't mean she was happy about it. Something precious had been lost, or perhaps had merely proved an illusion. Face to face, they didn't have a friendship at all, the way she'd felt they did when she'd been in Paris, and it would be better if she accepted the fact quickly.

It would be better if her heart was more obedient to the dictates of her head!

Feeling his stiffness and his distance, she still felt the same instinctive need to step closer, to touch him, to create a connection, skin to skin, which he was blocking today in the way he was speaking.

'How is she, anyway?' he said, staring down at the baby. 'Can I see her chart?'

He reached out without looking at her, and she handed it to him, making sure their fingers didn't touch. 'It's right here.'

'When was Dr Cassidy last here?'

'This morning, pretty early. I'm sure she'll show up again today.'

'*Thorough* is one way of putting it, in her case,' he said. 'Takes the pressure off me. She's been great.'

'She's very good.'

'What about Rebecca?'

'She's been having a lot of trouble trying to express her milk. Kit McConnell's spending some time with her, working on positioning the pump and trying to get her more relaxed.'

'Motivation's the real problem. Rebecca is so ambivalent about motherhood to start with. She's just too young, and there's no father in sight and no name been mentioned.' He began to study the figures on the chart. 'Numbers are good,' he said. 'What's Dr Cassidy thinking? Has she talked to you?' He looked at her finally, his eyes narrowed and distant.

'As of this morning, she was still pretty worried,' Emma said. 'She can still hear a murmur, even though it seems clear that the heart is pumping oxygenated blood. She'll send Alethea for tests on Monday, she said, and take it from there.'

Automatically, she looked down at the baby, who lay on her back with her thin little legs bent and apart, still looking like a frog. With her fine skin and absence of fat, Alethea usually looked quite red—darker than the flush on Emma's cheeks when she'd first seen Pete in the doorway.

Now, however, the baby looked pale and a little mottled, and Emma thought immediately, That's different. That's a change, even since Pete got here. Her lips are blue.

She looked at the monitor, and saw a change in the figures there, too.

'Pete,' she said, and reached out without thinking, to clutch his arm. It was ropy and hard and warm and tickly with hair, its solid bulk such a temptation to cling to.

For a moment he froze. He looked down at the point of contact between them, and she saw the tight, reluctant look on his face. He didn't think she was going to mention Claire, did he?

Emma dropped her hand at once, feeling as if her fingers were burning, and told him, 'Something's not right.'

She realised at once that she'd echoed the words Nell had been muttering at intervals since the baby's birth. 'She seemed fine a few minutes ago, Pete, but look at her now! She's turning blue.'

He looked, and swore under his breath. 'What's happening? What the hell is happening?' The baby was already looking worse. Drained of colour. Skin mottled with different hues, like a diseased leaf, lips and extremities blue. 'Is it her heart?' Pete demanded, clearly not expecting an answer. 'It has to be. Page Nell, Emma! Is this what she's been worried about?'

He flicked the earpieces of his stethoscope into place and grabbed the metal disc that dangled on his chest. Emma reached for the wall phone and stabbed with her forefinger at the two digits that would connect her with the A and E department.

'We need Dr Cassidy in Special Care immediately,' she said. 'Is she in the department at the moment?'

'She's with a patient,' said a female voice Emma didn't take the time to try and identify.

'This is urgent,' she said, not knowing if it was but responding purely to the frown, the tight mouth, the deep concern etched on Pete's face, and the changing colour of the baby.

'I can pick up that murmur, too,' he said. 'It sounds bizarre. Surely this isn't what Nell's been in doubt about? It's clearly not right, and she would have known that at once.'

'It's new,' Emma said. 'The baby hasn't looked like this before. The pallor and the mottled skin. And her oxygen saturation and respiration and heart rate are all falling. Her heart must be failing in some way that wasn't apparent before.'

'A heart defect that Nell didn't pick up? A heart defect made worse if that suspected patent ductus arteriosus is closing now?' He was talking half to himself. 'Dear God, are we looking something major? Hypoplastic left heart syndrome? Or…? Let me think. It could be that. There was another case I read about, just a year or so ago…'

Hypoplastic left heart syndrome was a very serious congenital defect, Emma knew, and invariably fatal without major surgery.

'Is that why she was small, even for her dates?' Pete was saying. 'Is that why she's been looking so good until now, because she's small enough that the PDA was maintaining adequate circulation? We've been medicating her to get it to close so the circulation pattern changed, and now that it's doing exactly that, we're in real trouble.'

'Is that possible, Pete?'

'Yes. As far as my knowledge goes.' He closed his eyes and shook his head. 'I'm not a heart specialist. I'm pulling this out of six different textbooks and a handful of case studies, and— But if that's what it is, it's going to be fatal without surgery, and without medication to keep the ductus arteriosus open until we can get her to— Lord, Sydney? Melbourne? Who does this surgery? Not many people, in this country. Nell will know, and I've been holding her back.'

'No, Pete, you haven't,' Emma said urgently, the unwanted need to touch him tingling in her hands again. 'She wanted to hold back, too. She thought the heart was probably fine. Lucy had a murmur, too, and she went home yesterday morning, thriving. Nell is as much aware of the social issues with the mother's lack of attachment as you are. And she didn't want to put the baby through unnecessary tests or transport if the heart was already doing its job. It's—'

'Nell! Thank goodness you got here so fast!' His exclamation cut off Emma's attempt to reassure him, and she had to stand back and listen while he outlined what had happened. His phrases were brisk, clear and decisive, but his fists were held tight. 'It fits the facts,' he finished. 'It fits what we know.'

'Yes, it does,' Nell agreed. She took a moment to think, the wheels in her mind turning almost audibly. 'If you're right, we need to treat her with prostaglandin E1, to reverse the closure of the PDA.'

'So we can do that?' He sounded intensely relieved. 'Yes,' he answered himself. 'If it'll work.'

'Obviously that's the only reason the heart has been functioning, fooling us into thinking everything was all right. Can we get the equipment in here to give her an echocardiogram straight away to confirm this? Then we need to get her to Melbourne. There's a surgeon at Royal Children's who does the procedure.'

'This can't wait, Nell.'

'No, it can't,' she agreed again. She pressed her hands to her temples, pushing back her dark blonde hair. 'We'll start the drug treatment straight away. We're going to lose her for certain if we don't. And maybe even if we do. Let me think. Is there a downside that I'm not seeing?'

'I would probably have picked this up *in utero* if she'd had proper prenatal care,' Pete said. 'It should have shown on a routine scan in the second trimester.'

'*I* would have picked it up,' Nell retorted. 'I'd have picked something up, if I'd given her the ECG sooner. I knew all along that something wasn't right, but with her healthy oxygen levels, I was leaving well enough alone…I didn't fully consider that it could be something this serious.'

'If we can't keep that ductus arteriosus open…'

'I know. We can measure her future in hours, or less.' Nell blinked. 'I hate this. She's come so far in other areas in just a few days!'

'And so has Rebecca, I think,' Emma put in.

'Can we get in touch with the surgeon straight away? They'll need to get the right team together,' Pete asked. 'If anyone's away…'

'Geoffrey Caldwell is the surgeon we want,' Nell answered. 'With Adrian Fitzgerald for the medical side.'

'Cardiologist. I've heard of him.'

'They're both very good, and they've dealt with this condition before, as successfully as anyone in the world. We have to get her that far first, get a medivac transport organised. Get her to Royal Children's alive.'

'Yes. That small detail.'

'Emma…?'

Both doctors turned to her, and the blaze of urgency in Pete's eyes drained the strength from Emma's legs. Was *she* the one who should have picked this up sooner? Could a handful of minutes make a difference to this baby's life? She hadn't realised that a patent ductus arteriosus could close so fast, or that it could have such grave consequences in the environment of a malformed heart.

'Prostaglandin E1,' she said. 'I'll chase it up. Is that all we can do?'

'It's the only thing that really counts,' Pete said. 'If we've read this right, that is. I'll get on the phone and start arranging a transport.'

'I'll get the ECG machine in here,' Nell said. 'She should go to Melbourne today, Pete, if it can be managed. Tomorrow at the latest. I need to think how else we can support her until then.' She pressed her fingers to her temples and closed her eyes.

Emma heard voices along the corridor, and recognised that they belonged to Kit and Rebecca. She took a deep breath.

'And one of you needs to talk to Rebecca about this,' she said. 'I can hear her coming now.'

CHAPTER FOUR

'YOU are cordially invited to Glenfallon's newest five star restaurant, Chez Emma, this Sunday at four p.m.,' read the invitation that Emma had created on her computer, 'so that I can show off my new French cooking and my French designer gown. Bring an apron, because you're going to help cook.'

Emma had delivered the invitations by hand on Friday morning—to Nell Cassidy's crowded office in the A and E Department, to Kit McConnell's lap as she sat at the post-partum ward nurses' station, and to Caroline Archer's microscope desk in Pathology.

Nell had phoned her acceptance to Emma's answering-machine that night, and the other two women replied yes on the spot, although Kit's acceptance was contingent on her fiancé Gian or her future mother-in-law Federica being available to look after her soon-to-be-adopted daughter, Bonnie.

'Why do we have to help cook?' Caroline had asked.

'Because that's the really fun part. I loved the cooking course I took in Paris.'

'But I'll taste everything, and it'll go straight to my hips!'

'You won't have time to taste much. You'll be making impossibly delicate julienned vegetables and stirring temperamental sauces non-stop.'

Sunday afternoon was glorious. Emma had shopped for her 'restaurant' on Friday afternoon. She'd been late getting off work the previous afternoon, following the drama of baby Alethea's newly discovered and potentially fatal heart condition, and concern for the baby's survival still simmered persistently in the back of her mind, dampening her initial enthusiasm for today's occasion.

Her months in Paris already seemed like a distant dream this afternoon, and the showing off of cooking skills and new hair and dress completely trivial in a way they hadn't even two days ago.

As certain as she could be without further testing that Pete's theory fitted the facts, Nell had started the drug treatment at once, and it had successfully reopened the rapidly closing ductus arteriosus. This had maintained the idiosyncratic but workable flow of blood through the baby's heart while an ECG machine had been brought in, confirming the diagnosis of hypoplastic left heart syndrome.

Arrangements were then made to transport Alethea to Melbourne's Royal Children's Hospital. She had been scheduled to fly out by plane in the hands of a retrieval team of trained medical people at five-thirty that same afternoon.

Rebecca had received the news of her baby's life-threatening heart defect with the same miserable ambivalence she'd shown all along. 'Is she going to be all right?' she'd asked.

'We hope so,' Nell had told her. She'd continued, 'At this stage, she'll probably undergo what's called a Norwood procedure. It's delicate and difficult, it will take seven or eight hours, and there are only a couple of surgeons in Australia who can do it. She'll probably need follow-up surgery in a couple of months, and she'll be in hospital the whole time. Count on three months, I'd say.'

'Three months!'

'I know. But you should realise that if you'd been born with this condition, nineteen years ago, you wouldn't have lived. The odds are a lot better now for your baby.'

As usual, Nell hadn't minced her words. Pete's face and voice had been softer, but he hadn't tried to pretty the picture either.

'We're very hopeful, Rebecca,' he'd said, 'but it's not like waving a magic wand. She may need further surgery over the next few years, and by the time she's grown up she may need advances in medicine and surgery which haven't happened yet. And you're going to have to take a crash course in courage. Alethea can tutor you. She's already working so hard.'

Rebecca had given a short spurt of disbelieving laughter. 'How can a tiny baby *work*?'

'She can. She has. You'll see if you watch her closely. She's survived! You have to believe in her, Rebecca.'

'Can I go to Melbourne with her?' Rebecca had blurted suddenly. She'd blinked back tears, and there had been something desperate and defiant in her tone. 'Is there somewhere for me to stay? There has to be! I'm her mother. I don't want to be so far from her. I couldn't!'

These were the words they'd all wanted to hear after their concerns about Rebecca's lack of emotional involvement, and Emma had spent some time on the phone, making arrangements for Rebecca's accommodation near the hospital.

Nell, the first arrival at Emma's, was in one of her snippiest moods on Sunday afternoon, and perhaps this was partly due to the extra work and worry she'd put in over the past few days with little Alethea.

'I hope you're not going to bore us with too much detail about Paris,' she told her friend. 'There's nothing worse than having people rave about their overseas holidays. Although I did enjoy your postcards,' she added, softening her statement a little.

'I'm not going to bore you with any details at all, Nell,' Emma answered calmly. She was used to Nell, whose bark was always worse than her bite. 'It's all experiential and visual. In other words, cooking and looking at my dress. But I want details from you first. Did Alethea's transport go according to plan? Have you heard from anyone at Royal Children's?'

Nell waved her hand tiredly. 'Let's not talk about that now.' Then she took a deep breath and started talking about it anyway. 'But, yes, she got there. I've heard from the cardiologist, Adrian Fitzgerald. She survived.'

'That's great. A positive step, anyway.'

'They've confirmed the diagnosis with another ECG, and they're doing more tests to map the exact nature of the problem. Every heart with that sort of defect is different. They don't want any surprises when she's actually on the table.'

'Heavens, no!'

'They're planning the surgery for Tuesday. Rebecca has settled in, apparently, and is spending a lot more time with the baby.'

'I can see you're still concerned, Nell.'

Nell laughed, then lifted her dark blonde hair off her neck, as if her skin needed air. 'You know me. Can't switch off. Would the baby's chances have been better if I'd looked more closely at that heart murmur straight away?'

'It wouldn't have made a difference, would it? You

focused on her breathing, and because of that she was stronger when she had to travel.'

'I suppose so. If only she'd had better prenatal care and a routine scan, then she could have travelled *in utero* because we would have *known*. That would have been safest of all. People don't realise—'

'No, they don't.'

'OK, we're really not talking about it any more. Distract me.' Her blue eyes darted around the kitchen. 'What's all this cooking I'm supposed to do? Give me my equipment and my recipe.'

They began to talk about marinades and glazes, and Kit and Caroline arrived. Caroline Archer was another of the notorious Sydney netballers from seventeen years ago, while Kit McConnell was a newer recruit to the group.

She had family connections in Glenfallon—a widowed aunt with whom she'd come to live. She and Emma had clicked quickly at work, some months previously, and she'd been a listening ear back then when Emma had needed to talk to someone about her fraught relationship with her stepmother, whose move to Queensland thankfully now looked permanent.

With Kit's recent engagement to obstetrician Gian Di Luzio, she'd instantly become a local girl. Emma hadn't had much of a chance to catch up with her since coming back from Paris, and she was eager to hear about Kit's future plans. How did she feel, for example, about taking on an adopted daughter as well as a husband?

'Oh, I've always wanted children,' Kit said quietly, with an expression on her face that Emma couldn't read. 'I already feel as if Bonnie is mine, and she has no memories of another mother. I know Gian's mother will be falling over herself to babysit, too.' She smiled.

Federica Di Luzio had cared for Bonnie at her family farm for more than a year. The adoption arrangement was new, however—part of Gian's brother's realisation that he had to make a permanent decision about his daughter's future. Mrs Di Luzio, too, had accepted that caring for her granddaughter full time was becoming too much of a strain at her age.

'It's not as if Gian and I will never have any time to ourselves,' Kit went on. 'This afternoon, for example, Gian's on call and Freddie has Bonnie at the farm. She'll stay the night, and I'll pick her up in the morning. After the wedding, we're going to swap. Freddie will live in Gian's unit in town, and he and Bonnie and I will live on the farm.'

'Is there a wedding date in your sights yet?' Caroline asked eagerly. She was a die-hard romantic about other people's weddings, although her own youthful marriage had ended in divorce some years ago, leaving her with a son who was now eleven, and 'not even the shadow of a man in my life' she sometimes said wistfully.

'We're stalking one, and about to go in for the kill,' Kit said, picking up on Caroline's hunting metaphor. 'Probably mid-November. The fifteenth. Pencil it in, but very lightly. It may still change. We may need more time.'

'Well, I've got the dress already,' Emma teased. 'So don't wait too long, or it'll go out of style.'

'Oh, the Paris designer creation that you wrote about in a postcard?' Caroline said.

'Put it on,' Nell ordered. 'I can't believe you were so extravagant, Emma!' She frowned sternly.

'Neither can I, but it was worth every cent. Or Euro, if we're going to be accurate.'

'Hmm. We'll see.'

'You will!'

Emma went to her bedroom, and did the thing properly. Swishy, silky, sparkling, *gorgeous* dress in dark wine red and black, heeled shoes, make-up she'd purchased and practised with at an exclusive Paris salon, and hair twisted up onto her head with a clip. How was it going to look?

She approached the mirror with trepidation, and saw the fatal flaw in the picture at once.

Yes, her ears stuck out. This was her lifelong, tragic secret.

For years, she'd hated them so much that she'd hidden them behind a thick, tangly perm. The stylist she'd consulted in Paris had been horrified at this, however.

'But, no, they're cute!' she'd exclaimed in French. 'Like a pixie. Believe me, I've seen far worse! And for this you keep your hair in that frizz? No!'

So Emma had obediently let her comfortable, woolly perm grow out and had returned to the stylist at the end of her Paris stay for a hair relaxing and conditioning treatment which had left it shiny and straight, and put her pixie-like-but-not-jug-handle ears openly on display.

Was it cute?

Emma took a longer look in the mirror, pressed her ears back against her head, then let them sproing out to their natural position again and studied them. There was no doubt on the issue. They really did stick out, but perhaps the stylist was right. They weren't nearly as bad as she'd always thought, and she loved all the things she'd learned to do with her new straight, silky hair.

Having been an absent hostess for more than twenty minutes, Emma hurried back to the three apprentice chefs, whom she'd left slaving over various tasks in the kitchen. The doorbell rang just before she got there, an irritant at that moment. She did an about-face in the corridor and answered it.

Pete Croft stood on the front veranda, dressed for the weekend in jeans, navy T-shirt and running shoes. His dark green car was parked in her driveway, and Emma saw two blonde moppets bouncing around in the back seat.

'Wow!' he said, stepping back a pace at the sight of her in the dress. He repeated himself in a slightly different tone. 'Wow.'

'Oh.' Having almost forgotten what she was wearing as soon as she saw Pete, Emma looked down, then smiled. 'I'm showing it off.'

'You certainly are!' Pete said.

Damn!

He immediately felt that he'd sounded crass and suggestive, which hadn't been his intention. He knew he'd been sending out mixed signals to Emma lately but, then, his feelings were mixed, which made it hard to do anything else.

'To some friends,' she explained quickly. 'It's from Paris. Part of my...'

She stopped.

'Transformation?' he offered, trying too hard to be helpful. 'Glenfallon isn't used to this level of glamour.'

'Makeover,' she said, then waved her hand. 'Hair and so forth.' She grinned, and looked like Audrey Hepburn, with those two little pink elfin ears. 'It's a girl thing. You probably didn't even notice.'

'I noticed,' he admitted, his voice rough. 'Your first day back. And it's obvious I've come at a bad time.' He turned and they both looked at his girls, who were climbing out the back windows of the car, one on each side. 'They've lost a favourite toy. A turtle. Green and brown, which means it'll be impossible to find if they've left it outside. I was wondering if it might be here, but I should have phoned first.'

'No, come in,' Emma said. 'I found a horse. And some aftershave.'

'Oh, Lord, that! That was a gift. I never use the stuff. I'm sorry. As for the horse…'

'A Lego horse. Please, come in, Pete.'

'Um…' Pete looked behind him again.

The girls were running around the car, about to get into serious mischief. Emma looked stunning, and for some reason this fact had muddied his thought processes totally. The dress clung to her like a surgical glove, baring her shoulders and her neck, wrapping her curves in a dark, shimmering caress. Her hair sat in a shining twist on top of her head, showing off a long neck and a clean jaw.

He could hear women's voices coming from behind her, inside the house. Emma's guests. Should he corral the girls back in the car and leave?

His hesitation on the issue was only keeping Emma here on the doorstep, he realised, and wasn't helping the situation.

'You look after your friends,' he said, finding his decisiveness at last with a deep relief. 'The girls can help me look in the back garden, if you don't mind. I know they were playing with it there. They had a sort of cubby house under the hydrangeas. Fairies live there, too, apparently.'

Emma laughed, and the sound was made of silver. 'I had a cubby there as well, about thirty years ago. I'm glad those bushes are inhabited again, because there definitely used to be fairies. I made them little green houses out of moss. Let me help you look.'

'In that?'

'In this.' She smoothed it against her body with grace-ful hands, and smiled.

Pete felt his groin tighten unexpectedly, and his heart give the painful little flip that he was getting used to. He needed moments like this so badly in his life right now—not the physical awareness, but the simple con-nection with another warm human soul—and there were far too few of such moments. Far too few people talked about fairies, and far too many people laughed purely out of cynicism and derision, never out of warmth.

'The dress'll be fine,' she added.

But will I? Pete wondered, still fighting her effect on him—fighting the part of it that he didn't want, the part that proved his unflagging maleness at a point when that sort of vigour had nowhere to go. He was still techni-cally married to Claire, his life still tangled with hers because of the girls. He wasn't free in any sense.

He called Jessie and Zoe and they tumbled into the house. He'd had a lot of trouble explaining to them why it wasn't their part-time home any more, and this visit would probably confuse them all over again, despite Emma's presence and her possessions reclaiming the space.

His heart gave another uncomfortable jolt in his chest. Where *was* home, for his daughters?

This was supposed to be Claire's week, but he'd had Jessie and Zoe since Thursday, when she'd announced over the phone, 'I'm too busy after the Canberra trip. I'll drop them off in half an hour, with their gear. There are some important developments that I have to take care of. People are depending on me, and I can't stop. I'll collect them again when the project is finished.'

What project? Had she received a promotion?

She'd evidently packed in a hurry, too, because she'd stuffed their backpacks full, and added an extra suitcase, but many of the items she'd included weren't things he imagined the girls could possibly need. Their best dresses. The complete set of books in Louisa May Alcott's 'Little Women' series.

In contrast, there'd been a dearth of underwear and socks, and he'd had to buy the girls some new ones. He didn't have a key to their marital home any more and, as he'd said to Jackie, he and Claire avoided talking to each other whenever they could.

On the way through the kitchen, out to the back garden, Pete encountered Nell Cassidy, Kit McConnell and a woman he vaguely realised he'd seen around at the hospital but didn't know.

'Dropped toy,' he said. 'Cooking smells good.'

They weren't staring at him, but they probably wanted to. He wished he hadn't come, and knew he'd counted far too much on finding Emma alone and getting an offer of coffee, or even a beer. Why hadn't he phoned?

'Hello, Pete,' Nell said, then added, 'You were right, Emma. The dress is *gorgeous*. You just need a white Rolls Royce to go with it.'

'I'd prefer a red Ferrari, I think.'

'A Ferrari is always a good look. The colour combination would be interesting, with that fabric.'

'Tell me later, in detail, guys. For now, I'm helping Pete to look,' Emma said, in his wake.

She was an incredibly good sport about it once they got outside, taking off her heeled shoes to pad around the garden in her bare, pretty feet, dress hem lifted daintily off the ground.

'Iridescent purple would have been a more useful if less realistic turtle colour,' Pete drawled.

'I know. It's not here,' Emma said, emerging from behind a forest of suckers which had sprung up beneath an ancient lilac bush.

She sounded a little breathless, and when she stooped to keep her piled, glossy hair from catching on an overhanging branch, Pete got an unintended glimpse...more than a glimpse...of the enticing shadows and slopes below the neckline of her dress. He took in a sharp breath, fighting to control his response.

They couldn't find the turtle. The girls stopped looking and started playing under their favourite bushes. It was definitely time to go. What was happening here? Why was this illusion of closeness, harmony and friendship springing up between himself and Emma again?

He'd given in to it the other day, telling her far more than he'd intended about his problems with Claire. He'd regretted his loose tongue almost at once. There was no place in his life right now for a female confidante. He had his sister for that.

He wondered how much he actually cared about the wretched turtle, and how much he'd seized on its loss as an excuse to see Emma so that he could mend fences a little and hopefully get back to the easier relationship they'd begun to build while she'd been away. He didn't want this awareness.

He didn't want to find himself backpedalling either. Backpedalling too far and too fast, the way he had when he'd so stiffly told her that it was dangerous to care about baby Alethea. He didn't want this new way that her body captivated him...The changes in the way she looked—her 'makeover'—that he kept trying to pinpoint were too powerful.

It wasn't the hair or the dress. She looked alive, and happy with who she was. It was new, he thought. She hadn't been happy when her stepmother had been living here, and she'd struggled through the death of her father before that, having moved home to help her stepmother care for him in his final illness.

But he couldn't afford to notice these things about her, couldn't afford to respond to them so strongly. He had to get things sorted out with Claire and the girls before he had any room in his life for even the glimmerings of casual male desire.

As for a new relationship…friendship, involvement, affair, it didn't matter what you called it… No! Out of the question! He was far too bruised and raw. He had to find a safe middle ground.

The repetitive thoughts kept churning in his head, with nowhere to go.

'We'll go,' he said aloud. 'If you do find—'

'Turtie!' Jessie suddenly exclaimed. 'Daddy, he's been hider-nating! Under a leaf!'

What a relief!

'Thanks,' he said to Emma.

'No problem. I'm glad he was only "hider-nating," and not permanently lost.' She gave that warm, dazzling Audrey Hepburn smile again, and he loved the fact that she thought a child's cute mistake with language was worthy of her amusement. 'If I find anything else…'

'You've got my address?'

'No, actually, I don't. You forgot to leave it.'

'Look, I'll phone and give it to you. I won't stop now. I've taken enough of your time.'

'It's fine,' she insisted, so they both stopped at the antique roll-top desk she kept on the enclosed back ve-randa-cum-sunroom and he scrawled it down while she stood beside him, frowning a little.

Pete made an adequately polite escape through the house with the girls moments later.

Did he think I meant I was showing off the dress to him? Emma wondered as she followed him to the door.

Her whole body had wrapped itself in coils of awareness that would have been warm and sweet and delicious if they'd been remotely appropriate. But they weren't appropriate at all. She knew his divorce wasn't through and, with twin daughters to bind them, it was possible he and Claire would still reconcile their differences.

Could Nell and Kit and Caroline detect the stiff aura of embarrassment he wore? It seemed to come and go, at the different times they saw each other, as if he couldn't find the right level on which to relate to her.

And it *was* embarrassing. For both of them. His erstwhile landlady—they didn't really have a friendship, for heaven's sake, they'd exchanged a handful of silly e-mails!—confronting him at her front door at four-thirty on a Sunday afternoon in a Paris evening gown. No wonder he'd been a little taken aback.

And then she'd made that stupid announcement about showing off, and it would have been hardly surprising if he'd thought she'd meant she was showing off to him. Had he guessed how aware of him she'd become?

'You should have invited him in for a cuppa,' said Caroline, after he and the girls had driven away.

'Heavens, no!'

'Dr Croft, right? He sends us his pathology, but I've never met him face to face. He looks nice.' Caroline paused for a second, then added, 'Cute.'

'He was a good tenant,' Emma answered carefully, then let her voice rise. 'But I don't want to talk about Pete Croft, ladies, I want to talk about my *dress*!'

They did talk about the dress, and her friends said the right things. Its purchase had been a form of therapy for her, and even cynical Nell understood that now. It was all about the pampered feeling she'd had while trying on creation after creation in the exclusive Paris boutique. The fuss that had been made of her as expert suggestions were made as to how it could be altered to fit her even better. The dizzy extravagance of handing over her credit card and thinking, I don't care how much it costs. Every moment of it had nourished her in some vital way.

Emma changed again into casual clothes, and the four women cooked and ate, listened to music and drank wine, laughed and talked, and she didn't think about Pete again until bedtime, after her friends had gone, at which point he pitched a tent in the camping-ground of her mind and wouldn't leave, even when she reminded him that his lease had run out.

What? Tents and camping grounds?

I must be dreaming, she realised, as part of the dream.

And since it was just a dream, and it seemed like a wonderful idea at the time, Emma let him pull her into the tent and kiss her deeply and sweetly, with no words, until they fell asleep in each other's arms.

CHAPTER FIVE

AT WORK on Tuesday, Emma paid dearly for the folly of letting Pete make love to her in her dreams.

With Lucy McNichol now safely at home with her mother, and Alethea Childer scheduled for her lifesaving surgery that morning in Melbourne, Emma was rostered on the post-partum side of the unit where Pete currently had a pregnant patient on hospital bed rest.

Liz Stokes was resigned to two or three more weeks in hospital. She was a local real-estate agent, part of the same agency through which Emma had rented out her house, and she was determined to keep involved in her business with minimal disruption.

Now aged thirty-six and taken by surprise with this, her first pregnancy, Mrs Stokes had been a heavy smoker for years. Although she'd stopped as soon as she'd discovered her pregnancy, the damage had already been done.

The fertilised egg had implanted low in the uterus, and the placenta had grown to cover the cervix completely. It was a condition affecting roughly six out of a thousand pregnancies, and was almost twice as likely amongst heavy smokers.

Liz Stokes had had a heavy but painless episode of bleeding in her fourth month of pregnancy, at which point an ultrasound had revealed the poor position of the placenta. At home, in the weeks that followed, however, she'd found herself unable to maintain the bed rest Pete had advised.

'I kept cheating to see if something would happen, but nothing did,' she'd said. 'So I cheated a bit more, and then…'

A second bleed had taken place, heavier and more dangerous this time. Liz had been rushed to hospital, needing a blood transfusion and intravenous infusion of fluids. Pete had refused to send her home after that, and a chastened Liz had agreed.

'I just can't seem to slow down, can I, Warren?'

'Real estate's a killer of a profession,' her husband had agreed. 'Liz was the top agent at Bryant and Wallace last year.' He was obviously very supportive of his wife.

Now, as Emma prepared to make a routine check of blood pressure, temperature, pulse and baby, Liz was surrounded as usual by laptop, folders, telephone, papers, pens and calculator.

'Sorry to disrupt your office hours,' Emma teased. 'But I'm here again.'

Liz laughed. 'I'd go nuts if I didn't have this to do. Our trainee agent at the office is cursing me, though. She has to do all my leg-work and my open houses. I got a new listing this morning, which she's going to just love!'

'Well, your blood pressure is good,' Emma said. 'Even if hers isn't destined to be. Shall we listen to the baby's heart? No one's brought the machine in for a few days, have they?'

'No, they haven't. Yes, let's, please!' Liz lifted her top and Emma slid the portable Doppler device over her taut, pale abdomen.

She was at thirty-five weeks now, and it had been seven weeks since the dangerous episode of bleeding. Every time she tried to get out of bed, however, she would feel pain and there would be minor bleeding, so they knew Pete's approach had been by no means too conservative.

The baby was now a good, healthy size, and Pete would probably order an ultrasound in a couple of weeks to check that lung maturation was complete, before scheduling the Caesarean delivery that was essential in a case of complete placenta praevia like this one. Liz, very vocally, could hardly wait for the remaining days to pass.

The Doppler crackled with static but didn't pick up the heartbeat both Emma and Liz were listening for. Moving the receiver higher, Emma heard the slower, louder beat of Liz's own heart, and Liz pricked up her ears.

'Is that it?'

'No, that's you.'

Emma felt for the position of the baby—head down, facing forwards—and adjusted the Doppler's receiver again. She massaged it quite firmly against Liz's abdomen, but still couldn't hear anything.

Liz was looking concerned. 'Why can't we hear it?' She sat up higher. 'It's been getting stronger all the time. We should be able to hear it, shouldn't we?'

Please, don't let there be a problem, Emma prayed.

There'd been enough of those lately, with Patsy McNichol's difficult delivery and small baby, and Alethea Childer's serious heart defect. Like most midwives, Emma preferred the warm, relaxed pregnancies and deliveries that produced healthy babies. Obstetricians might need to stretch their skills with regular challenges, but *she* didn't, thanks!

Although Emma knew that the foetal heartbeat could actually become harder to pick up as the baby drew closer to term, when its larger body sometimes blocked the Doppler's reception of sound, Liz's anxiety trespassed into her own rational attitude.

The baby had moved perceptibly, just a few minutes ago. There was no reason to suspect that anything was wrong, and yet…

'These portable things aren't very sensitive or reliable,' she said, but it sounded feeble.

'They're crummy,' said Pete in the doorway, and she turned, bathed in heat at once. He was clean-shaven, crisply dressed, hair still a little damp at the ends from his shower. He came forward with a brisk stride, confident and alert. If he was tired and stressed, it didn't show today. 'Can't you find anything?'

'No.'

He took the little device from Emma, and their fingers touched, just a brief brush, like cool paint. He drew his hand back quickly after the moment of contact, as if he'd noticed it and didn't want it.

I kissed him, Emma remembered.

Two nights ago, in her dream, with deep, lingering heat and silent passion.

She felt as self-conscious about it as she would have done had the endless kiss been real. The dream Pete had been a powerful enough presence, but the real man was even more so. He gave off an aura of confidence and authority and reliability that she knew she wasn't the only one to feel. Liz had relaxed markedly already.

'Let's see if we can get this thing to behave,' he said.

Behave? I need to do that! Emma thought. I can't keep thinking of him this way! It's got nowhere to go.

She stepped aside, to take herself safely out of the aura of his male body.

'Everything else looks good?' he said.

'Yes, her obs are all fine.'

'I'll measure the height of the uterus in a minute, Liz,' he said.

As Emma had done, he felt the position of the baby and placed the Doppler accordingly, then he fiddled with the controls, slid the receiver back and forth across the hard mound of the pregnancy and at last got a result.

'Thank goodness!' Liz said. All three of them listened for some seconds in silence. The beat was strong and fast and steady, over the persistent crackle of the machine.

'There you go,' Pete said, smiling. He pulled a tape measure out of the pocket of the doctor's coat he wore that day, and made a quick measurement. 'And he's grown. Not long now, Liz.'

'To you, perhaps! To me it still feels like half a lifetime.'

He smiled at both women once more, and then he left, and Emma hated the turbulence of her emotions in his wake. She couldn't afford to feel like this. It was clear that, even during the moments when he felt it too, he didn't want the awareness between them, and wasn't ready to act on it in any way.

'I'm such an idiot!' she muttered to herself as she returned to the nurses' station.

The phone rang just as she reached it and, after identifying that this was the post-partum ward, she heard Nell's voice. 'Would Dr Croft be in the unit?' she said in her briskest, coolest tone.

'Nell, it's Emma and, no, he's just left.'

'When? Because I phoned his surgery and they said—'

'A minute ago.'

'Can you chase him?'

I feel as if I already have been. Capturing his soul in my dreams, without his knowledge.

'It's urgent, Emma.' Nell's voice sharpened. 'I need him down here in the department right now.'

'Right. I'll go after him.'

She dropped the phone, gabbled an explanation to Mary Ellen Leigh and hurried to the stairs—quicker than the lift, since a glance at the lit-up number above it told her that it wasn't currently on this floor. She caught up to Pete as his car was about to turn left to reach the main hospital driveway, and she had to wave madly to get his attention. She was breathless when she leaned down to the driver's side window, which had slid down at his press of a button.

'What's the problem, Emma?' He leaned towards her a little, his shoulder tightening and his elbow resting on the sill.

'Dr Cassidy wants you in A and E immediately. I don't know why.'

They could both see the accident and emergency department's ambulance bay from where they were, and they could see a vehicle approaching. It wasn't flashing lights and there was no siren. It wasn't even an ambulance but a police car, and when it pulled in and the rear passenger door opened, Pete gave a shocked exclamation.

'That's Claire! Hell, what's wrong?' His dark-haired wife was weeping and struggling in the arms of the two police officers, clearly distraught. 'Nell must have been told she was on the way in, and wanted to...' He stopped.

'She did sound very concerned,' Emma said.

'Where are the girls?' He let go of the steering-wheel and pressed his hands to his head. 'Claire's supposed to have them today. I dropped them off there this morning. Where the hell are they if she's here, like this?'

'I have to go back to the unit, Pete.' Emma didn't even know if he'd been talking to her, let alone if he expected a reply.

'Yes, yes,' he said absently. 'Go.' His voice dropped to a harsh rasp. 'Dear God, what's Claire done with the girls?'

He was already reversing the car, twisting to look behind him as he manoeuvred the steering-wheel with one hand. He'd found a parking space between two other cars, but he'd approached it a little crookedly in his haste.

Emma opened her mouth to yell, You're going to hit. But at the last moment he veered again and got safely in, pulling the handbrake on with a jerk. The left taillight of his car came to a stop just a few inches from the adjacent vehicle.

Emma relaxed a fraction. Pete slammed the car door, aimed the key fob roughly at the vehicle and pressed a button. The car gave an obedient whoop, and he began walking rapidly towards the A and E entrance. As she watched, he broke into a loping run, his urgent, angular movements suggesting a strong and capable man at the end of his tether.

Emma could do nothing. She couldn't even watch him until he disappeared. She'd already stood here, frozen, for too long, and how would that help him anyway? How would this sick feeling in her stomach and this pounding of her heart be of any use to Pete now?

She had a newborn bathing demonstration to give in five minutes, and she didn't have any of the equipment set up yet. She would need to coax one of the three mums to attend as well, as Meg Snow had had a tough

delivery, under Gian Di Luzio's care, and was more concerned with her own aches and pains at this stage than
with learning to care for her big, healthy boy.

Emma gave her demonstration in a distracted state.
She was haunted, in particular, by Pete's distraught, repeated questions about the safety and whereabouts of his
daughters. Surely they would be all right! Was it possible that Claire could have harmed them in any way?
She'd looked so irrational and out of control, struggling
in the arms of the police.

Meanwhile, Meg Snow's one-day-old son Nicholas
did not co-operate with the bathing procedure. He cried
and kicked and was so slippery that Emma almost lost
hold of him twice.

Mrs Snow was critical. 'You've got soap in his eyes.'

'Well, as I explained, this isn't soap,' Emma answered
patiently. 'It's very mild and it shouldn't sting.' She
wiped the baby's red, wrinkled face with a soft cloth
anyway, although she didn't think he had anything in
his eyes.

Where were Pete's girls? What was happening to
Claire?

There was no message from the A and E department
when she'd finished the baby's bath but, then, she hadn't
been expecting one. Nell was hardly going to phone her
to gossip about Claire Croft's emotional state and the
reason for her dramatic arrival at the hospital in the
hands of the police. Issues of patient confidentiality
were, if anything, even more important in a growing,
community-minded town like Glenfallon than they were
in a large city, and the whole thing was none of Emma's
business.

That didn't stop her from thinking about it, however,
and from worrying about Pete and his daughters far more

than she had right or reason to do. Her Paris makeover hadn't been just in her appearance. It had been far more in her heart. She'd gone away thinking of Pete as a colleague, and she'd returned to discover that she'd…

Yes, admit it. Be honest about it. Look it in the face.

She'd developed a serious attraction, with a rapidity which frightened her.

At the end of the shift there was a message, and it was from Pete himself. Could she phone him at his surgery?

She did so at once, using the public phone in the main foyer as she didn't want colleagues to overhear, and she was put straight through. His voice was low, as if he also wanted to make sure he wasn't overheard.

'Listen, you need to understand what happened this morning, since you were there,' he said. 'You must be on your way home.'

'Just about. Pete, are the girls safe? That's what I've been concerned about all day. The rest is—'

'They're fine. She dropped them off at preschool, although it wasn't their session today. The teachers handled it. Now they're with me.'

'Oh, thank goodness!'

'Look, if it's convenient, you could drop in to the surgery. I've had a couple of cancellations. Hell, that sounds as if I'm slotting you in!' There was a rough, rusty scratch in his tone.

'It's fine, Pete. I'll be there soon. Not that you owe me an explanation, but if you want to talk… It's obvious that something's seriously wrong.'

'I'll see you in a few minutes,' was all he said.

When Emma reached the surgery, he was still with a patient. His girls were here, too, as he'd said, playing on the carpeted floor with the box of toys and books provided for waiting littlies. They recognised Emma, and Jessie said, 'You live in our rental house, don't you?'

'Yes, I do.'

'It's nice.'

'I have to work pretty hard sometimes to keep it nice. I did lots of painting before your daddy lived in it. It was fun, though.' She was rambling, in a vain attempt to cover her jittery state, but fortunately the girls didn't notice.

Pete opened his office door, and ushered out the elderly man he'd been seeing. 'I'll see you again in two weeks, Mr Carpenter, if you want to make another appointment now.'

He caught sight of Emma, held her gaze for a long heartbeat, then glanced around his waiting room and gave a little nod. 'Thanks for coming. Girls…?'

'We're hungry, Daddy,' Jessie said.

'And thirsty, too.'

'Mrs Meredith will…uh…' he wiped a hand around his neck and pinched his chin '…go over to the shops and buy you some chocolate milk and a banana each. Is that all right, Angela?' he asked in a quick aside.

'It's fine,' the older woman nodded. 'They're getting a little bored, I'm afraid. We don't have time to read to them. Old Mrs Paston tried, before she went in to see Dr Anderson, but then they started bouncing on her knees and—'

He winced. 'Right. Lucky nothing got broken. I'll try my sister again in a minute. Emma…'

His eyes blazed suddenly as he looked at her once more. She nodded, and smiled tentatively. His hair was a mess, as if he'd been running his hands through it all afternoon. His mouth was tight and tired. The energetic, freshly showered look from this morning had gone. He held the door open for her and she passed him into the room, feeling his heat and his tension.

He nudged the door shut with his foot, stepped towards her as she faced him and then pivoted on his heel to turn away again.

'Claire's been admitted to the psych unit,' he said, pressing his fingers to the muscles around his eyes. 'Nell Cassidy thinks she'll be diagnosed with bipolar disorder—manic depression, some people still prefer to call it—and from what I know of that illness, it rings so true I'm wondering why I didn't think of it before. I must have been blind! It came on gradually, I guess, but—'

'You're too close,' Emma said at once. 'Don't blame yourself. It's often like that. Sometimes it takes someone who—'

'I know.' He waved her helpless platitudes aside. 'But I'm a doctor.'

'And a good one, Pete.'

'Look, I wanted to tell you because you took that message from Nell when Claire was being brought in. You saw her arrive, and you knew how worried I was about the girls.'

'Of course you were...'

'This is going to get out, I imagine. It's going to be all over town, in all likelihood. She was nearly arrested in the park when she began taking off her— Oh, Lord, it doesn't matter what she was doing! But then the police officers realised that she was mentally disturbed. I didn't want you to hear about it at third or fourth hand.'

He sounded very stiff, as brittle as if he might snap in two. She didn't know whether to reach out and say, Let go. Talk. Cry, if you want to.

He looked as if he needed to, but also as if it would be the last thing he'd let himself do. He'd already shown her last week that he would close up, distance himself, if he regretted a confidence he'd shared. She had no right to push.

Instead, she said, 'You need someone to mind the girls this afternoon, obviously.' A concrete offer of practical help was often better than words, she knew.

'My sister's not answering her phone or her mobile.'

'Could I take them, Pete? They don't know me very well, but they know my house. You can collect them when you're ready. You probably need to see—'

'Claire? She won't. She's still very manic and out of control. I won't repeat what she said to me at the hospital, but Nell agreed it was best to wait until she's on medication and stabilised before I talk to her...before I even see her. There's a very good chance this illness can be controlled, and that she can live a balanced, normal life, if she'll accept that there's a problem and take her medication consistently. She's... You know, she's sensible in a lot of ways. I think she will. As for the girls, I can't ask you to do that.'

'You're not,' she pointed out. 'I'm offering. I want to, Pete. I want to do something. I care about you,' she gabbled. 'And it's only for a few hours.'

He looked at her, eyes narrowed, then let his face relax a little at last.

How had he taken that admission of care? Emma wondered. It was open to a broad interpretation. Should she have let it slip out, or kept it firmly in? She wasn't always good at hiding what she felt.

'That would be great,' he said. 'I should finish here by six. Or if I can get hold of Jackie—'

'Six is fine. Later, if you have errands to run. Save your sister for another day, when you really need her.'

'She'd appreciate it, I think!'

The girls were happy to go with Emma, and agreed to wait until they got to her place before they ate the bananas and drank the chocolate milk. Emma had correctly suspected that they'd get into a mess.

After they'd washed and snacked and washed again, she played hide-and-seek with them in the garden, and then they were happy to watch children's after-school television for an hour. Sitting cross-legged on her couch with their eyes fixed on the screen, they looked very young and so vulnerable.

They were just four years old, both blonde, but not identical. They were petite in build, and Emma wondered as she stood in the doorway, watching them, how strong they were in spirit. A child's resilience to upheaval was hard to measure. Even as watchful and caring a father as Pete might not know how his separation was affecting his daughters. Claire's newly diagnosed illness would add to their problems.

While the girls watched television, Emma made a spaghetti sauce. She felt like a witch, hoping to lure Pete into staying for a meal with the potent aromas of her cooking. The girls would need something nourishing, and she doubted whether he'd thought about cooking for them. When he turned up at ten past six, however, he brought potent aromas of his own in the form of two large, hot pizzas in square cardboard boxes.

'And in case the pizza is a nuisance, instead of being a way to say thanks...' he said, and held out a huge bunch of spring daffodils. He had a bottle of wine tucked under his arm as well.

'They're lovely. And the pizzas aren't a nuisance. I— I was hoping you'd stay, Pete.'

Emma took the flowers and hid her face by bringing them to her nose. They smelt earthy, sweet and full of pollen, and she knew she'd start sneezing any minute if she didn't take them away. But at least the heat in her cheeks had subsided a little. She'd been too honest with him today.

Pete smiled crookedly, his face tired, watching her reaction to the flowers. He took in a deep breath, the sound of it hissing a little between teeth he'd closed tightly together. She thought he was about to speak, but he didn't.

'We've got two dinners, actually,' she said quickly, 'because I made spaghetti sauce. But that will keep. Come in. You didn't have to bring any of this. Not as thanks, anyway. The girls have been lovely, and no trouble.'

They were still glued to their television show. The fact that they greeted their father so casually, barely dragging their gazes from the screen, was a reassurance that they felt at home here. Pete leaned over the couch to give them each a quick kiss on the tops of their heads. The fabric of his shirt stretched across his shoulders, and his dark trousers tightened across an already taut rear end. Emma moved deliberately away.

Straightening, he followed her through to the kitchen. 'I've got some beer in the boot of the car as well,' he said. 'Would you mind if I had one of those? Would you like one?'

Emma only very occasionally fancied a beer, but she instinctively felt that tonight should be one of those times. As a gesture of companionship, more than anything else. She didn't want to spout a whole lot of clumsy words of support. It would embarrass him, and would betray too much of what she'd begun to feel so strongly and suddenly. To join him in a beer, though, might be worth more than language right now.

'Lovely!' she said.

While he went back out to the car, she set plates and glasses on the table in the sunroom. No cutlery. Pizza was finger food.

And beer, according to Pete, had to be drunk direct from the can. He took several long gulps before he called the girls to the table, and Emma's gaze was drawn to his stretched, tanned throat and to the long lashes that fringed his half-closed eyes.

The pizza was still piping hot—pepperoni for the girls and Supreme for Pete and Emma. It was a very casual meal. Pete had brought lemon soft drink for his daughters, and Zoe spilled hers. Her father leapt up from the table before Emma could react. He strode to the sink, grabbed a sponge and wiped up the mess with calm efficiency.

'This is why I only ever put two inches at a time in their glasses,' he said. 'Zoe's elbows don't behave when she's thinking about something else.'

'Naughty elbows,' Zoe said.

'My elbows aren't *as* naughty, but a bit naughty,' Jessie came in, not to be outdone.

They were sweet girls—lively and imaginative, but never intentionally naughty. They didn't mention their mother at any point during the meal, and Emma wondered about that. What had Pete told them, if anything, about Claire's illness? Perhaps he was waiting for the right time.

Had he always been the steadier parent? The one Jessie and Zoe relied upon, and turned to? He was that sort of man. Not spectacular. Not the sort who needed to be the centre of attention, or the one who always got his own way. But he was as steady as a rock, as steady as the beam of a lighthouse in a storm.

And Claire was evidently the storm—the wild and unpredictable partner in their marriage. Was that what had broken the two of them apart? And if it all changed, once Claire was on medication and emotionally stable again, would their marriage have another chance? Emma didn't know how recent their problems were, or how long Claire's illness had been developing.

Her beer tasted over-bitter suddenly. It had gone to her head before the pizza could soak it up, but the light-headed feeling wasn't pleasant any more, as it had been at first. She knew that her growing feelings for Pete were feeding on dangerous illusions.

He ate largely in silence, and she didn't try to chatter. Let him have these few moments of relative peace. Let him enjoy the tasty mouthfuls of pizza and the refreshing, yeasty sting of the beer. She would have done so much more for him than this, if she could, but she knew it wasn't possible.

This man was still married.

The fact didn't stop her from offering him tea or coffee after they'd cleared away the meal, and he accepted a decaf.

As for the girls... 'I don't usually do this, and it's probably setting a dangerous precedent,' Pete said, 'but would you mind if I turned on the TV for them again? I just...don't have the energy for full-on parenting tonight.'

The weariness and strain were stark in his face for a moment, and Emma said quickly, 'Of course I don't mind. There's probably a sit-com on, or something.'

They sat at the table drinking their coffee, and without the girls there, chattering and unaware of deeper nuances, the silence between them was less comfortable.

Emma asked him, 'How's your new place? You

wanted to know about paint colours. Are you painting inside or out?'

'I'm getting some landscaping done,' he said. He looked relieved at her innocuous and relatively impersonal choice of subject. 'They started last week, and it's nearly finished. Paths and terraced stone walls, and a deck with a pergola out the back, which I'll want to paint.'

'It sounds lovely.'

'It's making the place look less raw. I thought I might cruise some garage sales and go out to the recycling centre at the tip, pick up a couple of old wheelbarrows. I'll paint them and plant them with flowers or herbs, soften the newness of the house a bit.'

'They'll look lovely!'

'I've never done any real gardening before. Know nothing about it. But I have this…' he frowned, then smiled '…deep itch to get my hands dirty, for some reason.'

Emma knew the reason, or thought she did. She'd felt the same six months ago, when her stepmother, Beryl, had finally packed up and gone to live with her daughter in Queensland. Capping months of manipulative, negative behaviour, she'd accused Emma of stealing from her, and Emma had thrown off the sense of obligation— that she owed her father's widow a home—and had called her bluff.

'Leave, if you feel that way, if you really think I'd do something like that,' she had said.

Beryl had left.

There'd been a sense of elation at first, followed by an equally painful sense of emptiness. Beryl's departure had taken away Emma's excuses. Faced with the rest of her life, Emma had found it lacking. She, too, had itched to get her hands dirty, make changes and complete projects that she could touch and see.

Sketching all this out to Pete, poking fun at herself a little, she told him, 'I went crazy around the house. Painted and decorated and gardened. Bought new furniture and linen. Tired myself out, but it was good.'

'You crave the healthy kind of fatigue, don't you?' he said, staring into his coffee. 'The physical kind, the kind that comes with achievement, instead of the drain of dealing constantly with impossible emotions.'

No. She wasn't going to let him talk about Claire. She was pretty sure he didn't really want to.

'You've picked the right season for putting in a garden,' she said quickly. 'As soon as your landscaping is done—'

'Hopefully this week,' he cut in.

'You can get things planted. You should phone up the local garden centres and get them to send you their catalogues.'

'Probably easier than dragging the girls round the garden section of the hardware store.'

'The hardware store?' Emma was shocked. 'You mustn't buy your plants from there!'

'No? Why not?'

'Go to the garden centre on Romney Road. There's a children's playground there, and even a café where they do light lunches and Devonshire teas. It's like an oasis, a slice of Australian bush and an English country garden, all mixed up together. The girls would love it, and there's much more choice, and better quality.'

Pete pushed his chair back. 'Speaking of the girls, I should check on them, because they're being suspiciously quiet out there.'

Emma looked at the clock on the kitchen wall and

found it was already after eight. 'Gosh, yes,' she murmured, but he'd already disappeared along the corridor in the direction of her living room.

'They're asleep on the couch,' he reported a few moments later. 'I should get them home to bed. Thanks enormously for this, Emma. I couldn't have gone straight home tonight.' He shook his head.

Suddenly, there was a heaviness in the air, and a sense of intimacy. Emma felt her pulses slow and begin to throb. She had put their coffee-cups on the sink a moment ago, and had been about to go through to the living room herself, when she'd met Pete coming back from his check on the girls. He'd stopped with his hand on the doorjamb, just a few feet from her.

Too close. They'd ended up standing too close, and here they still were, not moving.

It was dark outside, and his daughters had gone to sleep. No one would interrupt them. No one need ever know if they closed the small space between them and went to each other, touched and held each other. If they kissed. If they drowned in each other.

She knew he was thinking of it. The evidence was blatant in the soft glimmer of his brown eyes, and the way his lips had parted. It showed in the way he was standing. The hard male contours of his body softened a little, and he leaned closer than he needed to. Their bodies were like magnets, clamouring to draw together.

Emma could hardly breathe. There was no room inside her for rational thought about what should or shouldn't happen. They wanted this. She knew it. Wasn't that good enough?

But then Pete looked away, and drew in a rough breath.

'Gosh. Ten past eight,' he muttered, as if the clock

on the kitchen wall and what it said were the most important things in the room. The muscles in his tanned neck stretched as he craned around.

'Yes, is it that late?' she answered obediently.

'The garden centre idea that we talked about,' he went on. 'Are you free on the weekend at all? Would you like to come? You…uh…made it sound so nice, you should get to join in. If you'd like to, that is.'

He looked at her quickly, then looked back along the corridor, as if listening for the girls. He didn't dare to let his gaze linger on her face for long, Emma realised, because he knew exactly what would happen if they looked at each other again. He'd bend closer, his lips would part, and…

To help him, she began to inspect her fingernails, and tried to make her voice light. 'Are you looking for a tour guide?'

As he had done, she found herself looking up at him again almost at once, then looking away just as quickly, still feeling the softness in her face, the smile she wanted to give him and didn't dare.

'Yes,' he answered. 'I'll pay you in scones and cream.'

She wanted to ask why he was doing this. Why, when he wanted to kiss her and wouldn't, had he created another opportunity for them to be together? She might almost have asked the question aloud, because his next words answered it.

'It's a way of still e-mailing you, Emma,' he said. 'Is that OK? It's selfish. It's not giving you anything. I just…miss those e-mails. And I miss the sense of peace I had while I was living here.'

'I miss the e-mails, too,' she said. 'I've got an afternoon shift on Sunday, but that's not until three. I'll be your tour guide at the garden centre with pleasure.'

Their eyes met again. They both watched the kiss hanging in the air, and her face flamed. 'It'll be…yes, fun. Can I carry one of the girls to the car for you?' she asked quickly.

Pete straightened at last, pushing his hand against the doorjamb. 'Please. They'll probably wake up. If they don't, I might just put them to bed in their clothes tonight. Against the rule of good parenting, but—'

'It's good to break the rules sometimes.'

'Let me unlock the car, and we'll carry them out together.'

The girls didn't waken.

Later, in her bed, Emma herself didn't sleep.

CHAPTER SIX

'CROFT? Peter?'

The older doctor at the other end of the phone line was brisk. Pete didn't correct the other man's mistake. His name wasn't Peter, but of course most people assumed that it was. Generally, since he wasn't remotely fond of Pentreath—it had been his mother's maiden name—he let them do so.

'I thought you'd want a report on Alethea Childer's surgery,' Geoffrey Caldwell said.

'Yes, very much.' He had hoped to hear yesterday afternoon but hadn't, and would have called the hospital in Melbourne today if Dr Caldwell hadn't phoned.

'It went according to plan, and she survived. There's still a long way to go before she'll be out of the woods.'

Dr Caldwell continued with some technical detail that had Pete wincing as he considered what the atmosphere must have been like in Theatre, with the crowd of gowned figures bending over such a pitifully tiny form, using special extensions on some of their instruments to reach and manipulate the miniature chambers and vessels of the malformed heart.

He knew what the baby would look like now, too—attached to a tangle of lines and monitors, spread out on her back like a frog awaiting dissection, twitching with pain or with the effect of the medication that controlled pain, fighting to survive. How must it feel to see your baby looking that way?

'How's the mother?' he asked, when Geoffrey Caldwell had finished. 'Rebecca. How's she handling it?'

'Well, she's handling it. That's really all I can say. She's here. She's terrified and upset.'

'Lord, of course!'

'She needs a lot from the nurses. Sorry, that's my pager going off…'

Pete knew this was all he'd get for the moment. Geoffrey Caldwell was a busy man. He put down the phone and rang Rebecca's mother, who was at home. Rebecca had already spoken to her several times since the surgery.

'You were planning to go down, weren't you?' Pete asked, a little surprised that Susan Childer hadn't done so yet. 'I thought you were.'

'You have no idea!' she said, laughing wearily. 'I'm going to drive down tomorrow. Would have flown in the aircraft with them, only there was no room and I knew it would have been wrong.'

'Wrong?'

'Maybe it's still wrong. You see, if I go, Dr Croft, is Rebecca just going to hand it all over to me? The bonding, and the worry, and the love?'

'She might, yes.' He saw her point now.

'You know, when you told her about the suspected heart problem, and I wasn't there,' Mrs Childer went on, 'she made the decision to go to Melbourne all on her own. When she has to, she can handle this, and she loves that baby. But when I'm around, she turns into a child again, and wants to dump it all on Mum.'

'That's tough,' he said. 'I can see what you're saying.'

'But I'm that baby's granny, and I want to see her, so I'm going tomorrow. We'll just see…' Mrs Childer would probably need to go on saying those last three words for months to come.

Pete sighed and put down the pen he'd been fiddling with. Time to call in his next patient. His schedule had been delayed by Geoffrey Caldwell's phone call, and by Pete's own conversation with Susan Childer. He'd had a late start today to begin with, after visiting the psychiatric ward at the hospital on his way in.

The girls were at preschool again this morning—one of their scheduled sessions this time. Jackie would run them over to the childcare centre after the session ended at twelve-thirty, and he'd pick them up by six when the centre closed. If he was running late, he'd arranged for Vicki Lewis, one of the centre's part-timers, to bring them home. They'd have eggs for dinner tonight, that was easy, but he couldn't fall back on eggs or pizza every night of the week.

Meanwhile, the medication Claire had been put on to bring her down from her manic high had pushed her too far the other way, and she'd been sleeping since six o'clock yesterday evening, exhausted by the sleepless energy that had gripped her for days before. At least it meant Pete could see her, and talk to the staff, without unleashing an outburst from her.

By her bed, he'd brushed a strand of hair from her face and found a thin thread of tenderness still remaining, even after the roller-coaster they'd been on for so many years.

More than five years, in fact—since the day she'd told him she was pregnant.

'You have to marry me, Pete,' she'd said that day, quite panicky about it. 'I'm going to be a terrible mother, I know it! I'm not ready for this at all. I hadn't decided if I *ever* wanted children, let alone now. We hadn't even decided if we were serious about each other, had we?'

No, they hadn't.

He hadn't.

He'd just been humming along, thinking this was all rather nice and fun, but not looking to the future at all. Claire had been new in town, lively and attractive. And suddenly they were to be bonded together by a baby. Twins, as it had turned out. He'd found out the hard way that the future could sometimes arrive unwanted, all on its own.

Their marriage had been a mess from the beginning, although they'd both done their best for the sake of their daughters. Ending it was proving even worse. How long had Claire's illness been developing, while he'd already felt so hostile towards her after years of incompatibility that he hadn't picked up on it?

'Oh, Claire, I'm so sorry,' he'd whispered to her this morning, staring down at her sleeping form.

And he'd known he'd been right not to consummate the powerful awareness that had flared between himself and Emma last night.

The time might never be right for that, he realised. The weeks would pass, while the rest of his life was still an unsorted mess. The opportunity would slip away. The intensity of need would subside in one or both of them, leaving only awkwardness. He recognised this danger, but there was nothing he could do about it. He had to sort his life out first.

He stood up, left his desk and went out to the waiting room to pick up the topmost file in the pile that was balanced on the edge of the reception desk.

'Gwen?' he said to his next patient. 'Come on in.'

*   *   *

'I talked to Pete at lunchtime,' Nell said to Emma over the phone. She was at home, about to leave for an afternoon shift. 'And I heard from Geoffrey Caldwell directly, too. Thought you might want to know.'

About Alethea Childer, Emma realised.

At first she'd thought Nell might have been talking about Claire. She wanted to ask, but knew she couldn't. Professionally, it just wasn't her business, and Nell was the last person to break patient confidentiality. Pete himself might easily be regretting what he'd told her, as he had done before.

'The surgery took place, and the baby survived,' Nell said.

One piece of good news.

'That's great, Nell!'

There was a pause, then Nell said bluntly, 'Listen, is there something going on between you and Pete?' The Hippocratic oath didn't encompass any scruples regarding interference in her friend's personal life

'No. There isn't,' Emma said. 'I mean, I guess you could say we're friends, but—'

'I'm glad to hear it.'

'Why, Nell?'

Silence.

'Look, I know Claire's in the psych unit,' Emma said, then she sighed. 'OK, I—I guess I don't need to ask why, do I?'

'I suddenly realised I'd dug myself into a big, fat ethical hole,' Nell said. 'I'm glad you know about it. Steer clear. You don't need the grief.'

The advice sounded callous and cold.

'Don't you think *he* might need some support?' Emma said.

'People have to handle these things on their own. No.

I don't mean that, of course. Lord, I sound like my mother!' With whom, Emma knew, Nell had a difficult relationship. 'But Pete does have other people he can call on, and I just don't think you *or* Pete need an emotional complication of this nature when Claire's illness has pulled their divorce right off the table.'

'I told you there was nothing going on, Nell.' But Emma had to fight to keep her voice steady now.

Of course Claire's illness changed things. Hadn't she already understood this herself? She hadn't considered it quite in Nell's blunt terms, however, and Nell was right. Maybe there wouldn't be a divorce at all now. If Claire's undiagnosed illness was at the root of their problems, or even if it wasn't.

'Yes. Right. Good. Keep it that way,' Nell said. 'You looked fabulous in that dress the other day. We all told you so. Find someone who's in a position to appreciate the fact freely.'

'Nell—'

'I know. I'm a sledgehammer. It gets results. You've put up with it for fifteen years or more.'

'Because you're made of fluffy pink marshmallow deep below the thick outer crust, Dr Cassidy.'

'Not true,' Nell answered crisply. 'The marshmallow is, in fact, dangerously close to the surface and the crust is pitifully thin. Which is why I'm saying all this about Pete. You're a friend, and you need something nice in your life after the years you gave to your mother when she was ill, and to your father and Beryl. You don't need to get hurt. OK?'

'Does that prescription require a doctor's signature, or is it available over the counter?'

'Now, isn't that an appealing thought?' Nell drawled, and they both laughed.

The maternity unit was quiet, both in Labour and De-livery and on the post-partum side, when Emma went in to work. Liz Stokes had her two-bed room to herself, and the three new mums who'd been at yesterday's baby bathing demonstration had all been discharged, with their healthy babies feeding well.

One fourth-time mother had delivered last night, at around one in the morning, and the baby, the afterbirth pains and a stubborn uterus which wouldn't tone up as it was supposed to hadn't given her much rest since. Emma put a 'Do Not Disturb' sign on her door and left Mrs Eltham to catch up on sleep that she wouldn't get once she went home.

Emma wheeled the baby boy into the little nursery next to the nurses' station and kept an eye on him for the next two hours, cuddling him in the crook of her arm for half of that time when he began to cry. One-handed, she was still able to get through plenty of backlogged paperwork.

In the back of her mind, she wondered if she should cancel Sunday's arranged excursion to the garden centre with Pete and the girls.

Pete hadn't kissed her. She'd told the truth to Nell when she'd said that there was nothing going on. A kiss was surely the first step—sweetly melting mouths, warm bodies pressed together. Nothing concrete existed be-tween a man and a woman without a kiss.

Yes, but he'd wanted it. They both had.

In fact, they'd wanted it so badly that it didn't need to be mentioned and it didn't need to actually happen. She'd felt him and tasted him in the thickness of the air, in the look in his eyes. So perhaps she was kidding her-self. Perhaps intimacy did exist without a kiss.

She could easily phone and cancel the arrangement. There were plenty of potential excuses to do so.

But he very deliberately hadn't kissed her, as if he knew exactly how wrong it would be, and why. And he'd asked her to go with him to the garden centre as if their awareness of each other and his need for a haven of friendship away from the tumult of his tempestuous, failing marriage were two entirely different things.

If he'd kissed her, she might have been prepared to let him down. Since he hadn't, however, she let the hours pass, let her shift slip away, let the days go by, and didn't pick up the phone.

Sunday came, and once again the spring weather was gorgeous. Birds battled with the sound of lawnmowers to make their songs heard. The daphne had been out for weeks, filling the air with sweetness. It was getting past its best, and the soft, semi-translucent red and green shoots on the rose-bushes had unfurled into glossy leaves.

The citrus groves beyond the town were all in flower, and every breath of air was heavy with the sweet, bridal scent they gave off. Garden catalogues landed in people's letter-boxes, filled with impossibly bright colours and enticing offers of twenty per cent off.

Pete picked her up at ten.

He wore clumpy boots and thick socks and bare brown legs and khaki shorts. 'I didn't change,' he said. He wore a navy T-shirt and an Akubra hat as well, shading his brown eyes.

'No?' Emma arched her brows. 'I'd never have guessed. Thought you'd come straight from surgery.'

His laugh came unexpectedly, like storm rain on a tin roof. It was welcome to both of them. 'The landscapers finished on Friday,' he said. 'I had a load of topsoil delivered yesterday for the lawn out the front. I've been raking it out and putting in seed. Got up at six and left the girls asleep.'

'Earning your Devonshire tea?'

'Yep.' He grinned, and some of the strain had gone from his face since Tuesday.

Emma wanted to ask about Claire, even while convinced it must be the last subject he'd want to talk about. She couldn't let it go, though. It was too important. She touched his arm and asked, 'How's everything?' If he did want to talk about it, he could, and if he didn't, he could make his answer as vague as her question had been.

The touch was a mistake. She knew it at once, and dropped her hand, but it was too late. The imprint of his bare forearm lingered against her fingertips, bringing an awareness of warmth and hardness and a fine mist of hair.

'I took the girls in to see their mother yesterday,' he said quietly. The twins still sat in his car in her driveway, while he'd come by himself to knock on Emma's door. 'She was still pretty sleepy. She'd come right down after the full-blown manic state she was in on Tuesday. They hugged her, and she responded, but it wasn't a great visit. I'm not sure if they're still thinking about it. Just wanted to warn you, in case we get some odd behaviour from them today.'

'That's fine, Pete. I understand.'

'They're excited about this shopping spree, though. I'll probably indulge them. They want a garden like yours.'

'I'm not sure if the garden centre sells sixty-year-old hydrangea bushes.'

'Apparently hydrangeas are back in fashion, according

to my catalogues. We'll get baby ones and watch them grow.'

The girls were a little shy as they greeted Emma, and she didn't know whether to try and push past it or not. Every instinct suggested caution, but in the end she didn't have to worry about it. Pete put on a tape of their favourite performers, The Wiggles, and the car was filled with Greg, Murray, Anthony and Jeff singing about Dorothy the Dinosaur and Henry the Octopus, which meant that no one needed to talk.

The garden centre was already busy, and the girls ran around excitedly, examining plants and fountains and statues.

'Help!' Pete said. 'I don't know where to begin.'

'Trees?' Emma suggested.

'I'd like some shade,' he agreed. 'But I'll have to wait about thirty years!'

'Eucalypts and acacias grow much more quickly than that, but they limit what you can plant near them. A lot of European plants don't like what they do to the soil.'

'No?'

'You really don't know a lot about gardening, do you, Pete?'

'Told you I didn't,' he said cheerfully. 'But I'm ready to learn.'

'OK, then, lesson number one. If you're going to have Australian natives, it's best to keep them in one section, away from the rest of the garden.'

They wandered along the paths, examining a huge variety of plants, shrubs and trees and talking at length about Pete's garden. Then they pushed the twins on the playground swings for a while and talked about it some more.

It was such a lovely safe, easy subject, and they both

understood that. No undercurrents. No dark patches to trespass into accidentally and then burn with regret about for the next hour or the next week. It still had meaning, though.

Emma like the way Pete spoke about how he imagined the new garden when time had passed and things had grown. He wasn't afraid to use extravagant, poetic words. Some men had no descriptive vocabulary beyond the word 'nice', and seemed to feel that it wasn't *rugged* to talk about light and colour and scent. Pete could barely tell parsley from marigolds, but he had a feel for what he wanted, and if he didn't know the right word, he invented one.

'I like those frithy things,' he said when they'd finished in the playground and were walking around again.

'Yes? OK. Let's not buy the frithy ones, though,' Emma advised.

'Why not?'

'If you buy the ones that haven't quite frithed yet— the ones in bud—they'll do it at your place and look nice for longer. If you buy the ones that are in full frith right now, the flowers will have gone droopy and brown by the time you get them in the garden.'

'Can't I get them in today?'

'They should sit for a few days in their pots, to get used to their new home. And you have to prepare the beds and dig the holes.'

'I'm going to need more soil.'

'Definitely, and something to enrich it with. It all takes time, you know.' She frowned at him sternly, then added, 'They're azaleas, by the way. Which colours do you like?'

'Hmm, let's think…'

They'd loaded up two big wheeled trolleys with trees

and shrubs and seedlings and a stone birdbath and numerous bags of composted manure by half past eleven.

'It's going to be a lot of work, putting all this in,' she told him finally. 'Are you doing it yourself?'

'Not if you'll help me.'

'I'd—' she began.

'No,' he cut in. 'Don't answer.' He stopped and looked at her. 'I didn't mean that. Sorry. It just slipped out. You're already doing way too much. I'll get a bloke in, by the hour.'

'And you should probably test the acid balance of your soil,' Emma said quickly, as if she was thinking purely of Pete's garden, not Pete himself. As if this was so bone-meltingly *nice* purely because it was such fun to plan a brand-new garden, not because it was such an aching, important pleasure to plan a garden with *him*.

She would have helped him, if he'd really wanted her to. She'd been about to say so. She would have come round to his place the whole of next weekend and slaved for hours if he'd meant what he'd said, just to be in his company.

But he hadn't meant it. Perhaps he was a little more sensible than she was. And perhaps he had stronger emotions pulling him in another direction. Plenty of people felt attractions they never acted upon. This was just some time out for him. It was a necessary holiday from his problems with Claire.

'Let's eat,' he said. 'Let's pay for this lot and arrange to have it delivered. It's not going to fit in the car. The girls must be getting hungry, and I certainly am. Should we make it lunch?'

'Um, might as well, I suppose,' she said.

They had soup and a salad each, and the girls had

toasted sandwiches, but were eager for scones with strawberry jam and whipped cream as well.

'You need some, too,' Pete told Emma. 'With tea.'

'This is taking longer than you wanted, I'm sure.'

'And it's you that's holding us up, is it?'

'No, but—'

'Let me make the most of this, Emma.' His voice fell to a low, serious pitch suddenly, and the safe feeling— the pretence to each other, and to themselves, that they were just friends, and were just talking about gardens— shattered. Nothing about this was safe at all.

The sun shone on one side of his face, and he'd let his legs jut out sideways. His knees were brown, and a little soil-stained. Beneath the tilted brim of the hat, his eyes sat in shadow, but Emma could read more than just his eyes. She could read every movement he made.

'You've got something in your hair,' he said, and reached across the table. 'Lean forward a bit, and sit still.'

He barely touched her, just pulled a shrivelled leaf from her hair. She felt the light brush of his wrist against her temple, and watched the flick of his fingers as he tossed the leaf away. There was a stillness to the moment that made it seem to last much longer than it really did.

And he didn't kiss me, so it's all right, she thought later, after he'd dropped her home so that she could get ready for work.

He'd thanked her warmly, but he hadn't touched her, and he hadn't got out of the car. Perhaps because he'd known that if he did...

He *would* have kissed me. He wanted to.

Emma touched her fingers to her lips, and felt the soft pressure of his mouth as vividly as if it had been real.

She closed her eyes, tasting him, feeling him, and aching all over.

He would be home by now, awaiting the delivery of his plants. Minutes had passed since he'd driven away, but her mouth was still sensitised and expectant after the flash of opportunity in the car when it could have happened—the moment when he'd thanked her, and she'd had her hand on the doorhandle, and they'd been looking at each other, and it would have been easy for him to lean across and brush her lips with his. The moment when, because the girls had been watching, it could have been brief and light and would barely have meant anything at all.

But Pete hadn't even done that.

So it was all right.

No betrayals, no complexities, no promises, no illusions.

Five days passed.

Liz Stokes had reached what she'd begun to call 'the magic thirty-seven-week mark' and was due to go down to Radiology for her ultrasound scan today. She was impatient about it.

'If it looks good,' she asked Emma, 'would Dr Croft do the Caesarean today, do you think?'

'Probably not,' Emma answered. It was already two o'clock. Caesareans were usually done in the morning, and Friday wasn't the best day, in any case.

'Because the weekend is coming, right?' Liz guessed. Her tone was bitter and frustrated. 'If he was in real estate, he'd *really* know what working all hours means, and every weekend. I don't know why doctors complain! I'm going to tell him I realise he's only protecting his golf game.'

Emma resisted the urge to sketch out Pete's far more serious problems at home, and his need to spend time with his daughters.

'It's more than that,' she told Liz instead. 'Certain hospital departments aren't staffed so fully on weekends. Pathology and Radiology, for example. If you or the baby needed extra tests or treatment, we might have to wait while extra people were called in.'

'That's ridiculous!' Liz snorted. 'Babies are born naturally on weekends all the time!'

'Don't give that little boy of yours any dangerous ideas,' Emma teased. She could understand Liz's short temper after so many weeks of bed rest.

In the event, Pete's unforgivable decision to schedule a weekend for himself didn't enter into the matter. Liz went down for her ultrasound, endured an uncomfortable wait with a full bladder as Radiology was running behind, and then returned to await Pete's verdict after he'd looked at the scan and read the report.

He phoned the news to Emma in the late afternoon.

'Tell Liz I'm sorry, but I think we should wait a couple more weeks,' he said. 'The baby's still pretty small, possibly as a result of the bleeds she had earlier in the pregnancy. I'd hate to deliver him and have him end up in Special Care.'

'She's not going to like this.'

'I know. *Now* she isn't. But I'm not looking at now. I'm looking at the rest of the little guy's life.'

'I'll break the bad news.'

'Before you go…'

'Yes, Pete?' Oh, hell, it was ridiculous! Just the tiny change in his tone had set her heart thudding!

'I've got my garden bloke for the weekend, but he's made it clear he's just the brawn. He'll cart dirt—in fact, he's doing that today—and he'll dig holes, but he won't decide on where to put things.'

'You want me after all,' she blurted, careless in her choice of words.

'I...uh...always wanted you, I just didn't think I had the right to ask if you could,' he answered.

There was a thick silence. Emma could almost hear him wondering how to escape gracefully from a trap of language use that they'd both helped to create. The double meaning was as clear as subtitles on a screen. He wanted her, and she wanted him.

She took a breath and said, 'I'll bring my gardening books and some of my tools. What time to do you want me? What time should I get there?'

'Well, my bloke's an early bird.' She could hear the roughness and the struggle in his voice, even on the phone. 'He likes to start at seven-thirty.'

'Ugh! On my day off!'

'Yes, I know. Don't come that early.'

'How about eight-thirty? Is that early enough?'

'Perfect! I'll give you breakfast. Croissants, or something.'

'Yum.'

As expected, Liz wasn't happy about Pete's verdict on the ultrasound. 'How much difference can a couple of weeks make?'

'A lifetime, Liz,' Emma said seriously. 'Most babies born at thirty-seven weeks will do fine, but occasionally there can be a problem. Even at very low odds, do you want to take any kind of a chance on your baby's long-term health?'

'No, none,' Liz agreed. 'You're right. It's not worth any risk at all. I'll wait. But don't leave any sharp objects within reach, because I might start throwing them!'

*   *   *

Emma got to Pete's at twenty to nine the next morning.

His 'bloke', an older man named Darryl with crooked teeth and a smoker's cough, was emptying barrowloads of sand into the shadecloth-canopied sand-pit Pete's landscapers had made for the girls. Jessie and Zoe jumped up and down, wanting to play in it straight away before it was even full.

They had sticky, jam-stained mouths, having apparently just finished their croissants, and to Emma's surprise and pleasure, they both ran up when they saw her, wanting to give her kisses. Did they like her that much, then? She could so easily get deeply attached to them. She bent down and hugged them, and got jam and sand on her cheeks. It set like cement at once.

'Somehow,' Pete drawled, meeting her on his way out the back door, 'I don't think your sticky face is because you've already eaten. Want to go and wash?'

He led the way inside.

'I'd better. They won't think I'm washing off their kisses, will they?'

'They won't notice.' He stopped in the middle of the bright, modern kitchen. 'They're a bit funny this morning. Claire was discharged yesterday, and she's gone to Canberra to stay with her mother. She'll be seeing a psychiatrist there. It sometimes takes a while to get the medication right, and to work out just what's going on— whether there are emotional triggers that are important, all sorts of things.'

'Do the girls know?'

'Yes, I've told them. It seems to have made her absence more real to them. Mummy's gone to stay with Granny in Canberra while she gets better. They wanted to know why they couldn't go, too, to help look after her.'

'Was it a possibility?' The stickiness on her cheeks pulled and tightened every time she moved her face. It was irritating—trivial yet distracting, when Pete was talking about something this important and she was so desperate to give him the right attention. 'That they might go, I mean.'

'Claire thought it best not to have them with her,' he said. The low pitch of his voice seemed to enclose them in greater intimacy. 'She felt it wouldn't be fair to them. She doesn't have much energy or focus for them at the moment, and felt they wouldn't be safe in her care. I couldn't disagree, after the way she's dealt with them recently. Effectively, they'd be her mother's responsibility, and since the goal is for Hester to help Claire learn to manage her illness…The girls are better off here, but they're missing her today.'

'Pete, I haven't been asking you much about all this,' Emma said. 'I've felt perhaps you didn't want to dwell on it. But, please, remember that I'm here.'

'I do,' he said quietly. 'I remember it every day.'

He turned to the sink and picked up a dish mop, waved it in his hand then looked at it with a frown on his face, as if he couldn't remember what it was for.

'I'm glad, Pete,' she said, her voice too husky.

He dropped the mop again. 'Hey, want those croissants and some coffee, once you've washed?'

'And get my face sticky again straight away? Yes, please!'

When Emma had her coffee and a croissant in hand a few minutes later, Darryl finished filling the sand-pit and needed his next instructions.

'Turn the composted manure into the soil, water the beds and cover them with mulch,' Emma decreed. 'It's easier to mulch first and plant second. We can scrape the mulch aside to dig the holes.'

'I'll open the bags of compost,' Pete said. 'Do you want to think about where we're putting everything, Emma? You're our expert today.'

The plants, trees and shrubs he'd bought last weekend made a colourful miniature forest in the angle of newly paved space between the deck and the house. As instructed by Emma, he'd watered them every couple of days, and they were all doing well. She contemplated them thoughtfully, trying to imagine how they'd all look months or years from now, when they were grown.

Hard! Almost as hard as trying to imagine her own life several years down the track.

The girls ran back and forth between the garage and the new sand-pit, bringing their sand toys. Pete began chopping open the thirty-litre bags of composted manure with the edge of a shovel, and Darryl raked out the contents and turned the soil over, spreading the rich, dark stuff evenly.

Emma worked out which way was north, and which parts of the garden would get direct sun at which times of day. They'd roughly planned where to put the five young trees Pete had chosen, so she put down her coffee and the remaining end of her croissant and carried the trees into position, one by one.

When she got to the last one, Pete took a break, leaning on his shovel, and watched her. Self-conscious as always, she asked him, 'Here, Pete?'

'Maybe a little closer to the fence?'

'It'll grow, remember, and this one'll spread out sideways, too.'

'You're right. We're keeping all the Australian natives in this area, aren't we?'

'Yes, and we'll put the…'

She stopped. Zoe had suddenly fallen on the cement in her eagerness to bring another load of toys to the sand-pit. She was crying loudly. Pete ran to her at once, took her up in his arms and sat down on the new garden wall.

'Ah, sweetheart,' he crooned. 'Did you trip?'

'Ye-es.'

Emma came over and he said to her, 'She's got some grazes on her knees and arms. Not deep ones, but they're bleeding. Could you bring a bowl of warm water from the kitchen, and a towel to pat them dry?'

'Dressings?'

'There's a packet in the medicine cabinet in the main bathroom. We'll use a couple to cover the worst spots.'

Zoe was still crying when Emma got back with the things Pete had asked for. Jessie looked on, round-eyed, while Pete washed the grazes clean and patted them dry. Putting the sticky bandages on, he managed to comment to Emma, over Zoe's head, 'It's psychological more than anything.'

'Is it?'

'My kids have an unshakable faith in the power of little bits of flesh-coloured sticky plastic, with squares of gauze attached, to alleviate pain immediately.'

'Faith is good,' Emma said.

Zoe's sobs tapered away. 'I want Mummy,' she said in a very small voice. 'Why isn't she here?'

'We've talked about that, love,' Pete said gently. He kissed the top of her head. 'She's gone to Canberra to stay with Granny. She's not feeling very well, and Granny's going to look after her until she gets better.'

'*We* could look after her.'

'We could put bandages on her,' Jessie agreed.

'She doesn't have a bandage kind of sickness. She has a different kind of sickness that needs some time and lots of quiet. Do you want to draw pictures to send her later today?'

'Now!' Jessie said. 'I want to draw one now.'

'Now, this minute?' Pete said.

'Yes! Yes!'

'Drawing it is, then.' As an aside, mostly to Emma but partly to himself, he added, 'Am I spoiling them? Is that going to be the result of everything that's happening? I find I'm jumping to give them everything they want, the moment they want it.'

'I—I don't think that's something you should think about now, Pete,' she answered him helplessly.

Both girls had apparently forgotten all about the new sand-pit and the grazed knees and arms, and Pete had to set them up with drawing things at the dining table inside. His face wore a little of its familiar bleak look when he came out again, but he shook it off quickly. Emma could only guess what an effort it must have taken to do so.

They didn't finish in the garden until five-thirty, after a break for a sandwich lunch on the deck. Darryl had knocked off an hour earlier, at half past four.

'We've done well,' Pete commented, surveying several mulched beds, where hopeful, green-leafed young shrubs were flowering their little hearts out in a late afternoon breeze. Some of them were already in the ground, while other sat in their pots, marking their future positions so that Pete could plant them the next day.

'We have,' Emma agreed. 'Not to downplay Darryl's role as the brawn.'

'Or the girls, because they've put up with not getting much attention today.'

'They're going to love watching all this growing up, and helping you to keep it watered over summer.'

'You'll stay to eat, won't you?' Pete said, his voice dropping to the more intimate pitch that she recognised easily now.

She moved away before she answered, bending to cradle a pale apricot azalea blossom in her hand. 'That'd be nice,' she said, with her back to him. 'I don't have much in the fridge at home.'

'It'll be simple. We'll barbecue some sausages and chops. There are salad fixings in the kitchen, and I've got a bag of oven fries I can throw in.'

'As long as it's food!'

'Sounds like you're hungry already. Would you like a drink? Wine? We can have some biscuits and cheese to keep us going while I fire up the grill.'

'Would the girls like a bath? They got much dirtier than we did, even though I'm quite sure we did more work!'

'Happens with kids, for some reason. They're dirt magnets. And they'd probably love a bath. Are you up to it? I read an article recently, quoting a study which claimed that bathing children uses up more calories than... Can't remember...playing tennis, or something.'

'More calories than planting a garden?'

'Try it and see. Yell, if you need help. Their towels are on the rail, and you can put them straight in their jammies, because they're going to bed early tonight. I'll get the barbecue started.'

The girls got themselves undressed while Emma ran the bath, pulled out some bath toys and got the water temperature right. She held their hands as they climbed in, afraid that the porcelain tub might be slippery. It was an awkward climb from the floor for little legs.

They seemed quite happy to accept her help, and to be left for a moment, with the taps still running and clear instructions not to touch them, while Emma dashed across the corridor to the laundry to dump their dirt-stained clothing in the washing-machine.

The laundry window was open, and she could hear the click-click-click of the barbecue's automatic ignition outside as Pete got it going, while the sound of the bath water threatened to swamp the clicking noise from the other direction. They were two such domestic, family-oriented sounds, and they fed the dangerous needs that were growing inside her.

Hearing a loud splash, Emma hurried back to the bathroom, knowing that she, rather than Jessie and Zoe, was the one who risked getting in way out of her depth.

CHAPTER SEVEN

IT WAS peaceful on the deck—that blessed peace so important to Pete at the moment, and which was sourced in such very simple things. He could smell the resinous aroma of the pine bark mulch he and Emma had spread thickly on top of the new garden beds, and the moist, peaty odour of the enriched soil.

The barbecue grill plate had heated up to the right temperature, so he slid a little oil over it, covering it evenly, and tossed on the meat and the sliced onions. Their smell quickly vanquished the other scents in the air.

The late sun fell on his back like a big, warm hand. It might be just light enough and mild enough for them to eat here on the deck tonight.

Emma appeared.

She had wet patches on her pink T-shirt, making it cling even more closely to her body's very feminine curves, and there were some damp strands hanging in her silky hair.

'Looks like you got at least half of a bath as well,' he said.

She laughed, a little breathless. 'You weren't kidding about burning up the calories,' she said. 'But it was fun. We had a pretend tea party, and I washed their hair.'

'That's always a major undertaking. How's the floor?'

'Awash. Should I mop it up?'

'You'd better, if you don't mind,' he said. 'Those big, smooth tiles are slippery when they're wet. Jessie had a fall in there last week, and I've been pretty careful about it since. There are a couple of old towels in a box in the laundry cupboard. Use them to soak it up.'

'This smells great, by the way. I'm starving!' She grinned.

'I don't have a blow-drier for your hair. I'm sorry.' He reached out and tucked the wet strands back behind her shoulders, out of the way.

As usual, even such a tiny gesture at once seemed too personal, too significant. It cut immediately through the pretence that this was just a friendship—a pretence which, thankfully, she seemed to understand the need for just as he did. He dropped his hand again straight away.

Let me…' she took in a fluttery breath '…check on how they're going with brushing their hair.'

She turned and disappeared back inside, and he heard her calling, 'Girls, do you need some help?'

Pete liked Emma's energy. It was positive, happy, productive. So different from Claire's, he couldn't help thinking. It wasn't just Claire's illness. For as long as he'd known her, she'd had a way of exhausting herself and the people around her.

With Claire at the helm, Jessie's and Zoe's bathtimes had been fraught occasions, full of scolding about water on the floor and exaggerated fears about the hygiene of bath toys. Claire had flatly refused to wash their hair at all.

'I can't stand it!' she'd said. 'They cry, and if I give them a towel to put over their eyes, they drop it in the water. I don't have the patience!'

Pete had always done it. He hadn't minded, hadn't made a big deal of it, but it was a nice change to see

Emma covered in water instead of himself, and she seemed so cheerful and relaxed about the whole thing.

There was nothing relaxed in the way he felt about her. The issue was building to breaking point between them. He sensed this, but couldn't do anything about it. He had no idea what the future held.

And the sausages were starting to burn, he realised. He turned them over, tossed the onions around on the grill plate, then poured out two glasses of wine.

'Sit down,' he told Emma when she came back out. 'You let me work you too hard today.'

'If you like, I'll let you send me home without my helping to clear up,' she offered with her impish, Audrey Hepburn smile.

He laughed and, Lord, it felt good!

It felt so good that Pete began plotting the means to see Emma again as soon as she'd gone home that night. He knew that their meetings had to keep within certain boundaries for the foreseeable future, even though he very carefully never framed in his mind quite what those boundaries were.

Who was he protecting? he occasionally asked himself.

The answer always came with a groan and a roll of the eyes. Who *wasn't* he protecting?

Claire was too emotionally fragile to deal with a new woman in his life, when their divorce wasn't yet finalised. Jessie and Zoe didn't need any more confusion and uncertainty. They didn't need to wake up thirsty one night and flit into his room, wanting a drink of water, only to find a new woman in their father's bed…no matter how much their father might want to have her there.

And Emma deserved better than to be merely an additional and ill-timed complexity in his already fraught schedule. She deserved to be offered his heart in a far more complete, unfractured and certain state than he could possibly offer it at the moment.

All of this was obvious and true and sensible and right.

But then a very male and ego-driven part of him would put in a powerful counter-argument to this scrupulous consideration of other people's needs.

What about me? When do I get a chance to have some needs—not to mention some fulfillment—of my own?

So he constructed various rules to govern his conduct with Emma, and pretended to himself that he was doing the right thing.

Seeing her in the hospital cafeteria was fine, for example. It was an attractive place, belying to a certain extent people's cynical notions about hospital food. Its large windows, overlooking the river, definitely helped, and the menu had changed a lot since the place was opened ten years earlier. Curries were no longer a way of using up the leftover meat from yesterday's roast, and sandwiches didn't just come in the form of pre-sliced white bread or spongy, over-aerated rolls.

Wasn't it reasonable, he told himself, if he should stop for lunch or an evening meal there occasionally, if he'd had patients to see at the hospital, and if the girls were with his sister or at childcare?

It wasn't so reasonable that he only made up his mind to eat there once he saw that Emma was in her usual spot over by the windows, but to hell with such scruples! This way, he managed lunch with her on Tuesday and dinner on Thursday, and they talked quietly about the garden, the girls, the movies that were currently playing in town.

'Yes, I've heard that's good,' she said about a British film which had opened the previous week.

'Could we fit it in on the weekend, do you think?' he suggested.

'Mmm, probably. I've got an early shift on Saturday.'

'Saturday night, then. I'll get Vicki from the childcare centre to babysit. Do you mind if it's the late session? Ninish, I think it'll be, once Jessie and Zoe are asleep. I want to spend as much time with them as I can.'

'That's fine. We can meet at the cinema.'

'It'll be my treat, of course.'

Meeting at the cinema was pretty safe, Emma felt. It was crowded, a modern quadriplex, with different movies screening in each auditorium and staggered starting times. An American action film was just letting out when they arrived on Saturday night, flooding the foyer with teenagers and young couples, so she first caught sight of Pete across a sea of heads.

'Got you!' he said, when they finally reached each other. 'For a moment, I thought you were going to get swept out with the tide.'

'So did I.'

He squeezed her hand, and she returned the pressure briefly. His palm was warm and dry, and her smaller hand was lost inside his. But they both let the contact drop almost at once. Breaking the rules. Pushing the boundaries. They didn't need to talk about it. Talking about it would break the rules as well.

A couple brushed past them, on the way out of a previous session, and the woman smiled and said hello to Pete. 'Nice to run into you,' she told him, and her glance flicked across at Emma, betraying her curiosity.

Pete hesitated for a moment, then said, 'Emma, this is Mandy and her husband, David. Mandy's a friend of

Claire's. Mandy, this is Emma, a colleague from the hospital.'

'Hi!' Mandy's smile was brittle and brief. 'Are you a nurse?'

'A nurse-midwife, yes.' Emma felt an urge to explain further, like the point of a sharp stick prodding her in the back.

We're just seeing a movie. Nothing's going on. You can phone Claire in Canberra and tell her, if you want, because there's nothing to tell.

But she resisted it. She was probably imagining Pete's discomfort and Mandy's suspicion. Still, she was relieved when Mandy and David continued toward the cinema exit. Pete watched them for a moment, then turned away, the movement decisive and deliberate.

'I've got the tickets,' he said. 'Do you want something to eat or drink?'

Not tonight. Her stomach would have rebelled. It felt far too fluttery. 'No, thanks,' she said. 'I'm fine.'

'You're less expensive than the girls, then!'

'We should go in. I hate finding a seat when it's dark.'

'There'll be plenty of room. This crowd's come for alien battles in Cinema Three, I think.'

He didn't tell her that she looked nice, in her flowing skirt and neat, long-sleeved pastel top, but, then, she hadn't expected him to. A comment like that would have skirted the edge of safety. *He* looked nice, achingly so, in dark trousers and a casual cotton knit sweater over a paler collared shirt.

The movie was good, and funny. Emma realised how little she'd heard Pete laugh, and never this thoroughly and freely. It was a rich sound, and it warmed her. He deserved to laugh this way more often. If he was having a good time tonight, she was happy. If he was only letting himself do this because he had her with him to keep him company and provide him with an excuse to let go, she was even happier.

When he shifted in his seat, she could feel his movement, and sometimes the slight pressure of his arm. She wanted to lean closer, feel the strength and the warmth of his arm muscles, solid and relaxed against hers. She wanted to smell the reassuring scent that clung to him— a mix of soap and sun-dried clothes and male skin. But her awareness of the unspoken rules between them got in the way once again, and she stayed where she was.

'Did you like it?' he asked, when the credits rolled at the end and the lights came on.

'Yes, I did. And you, I don't need to ask. If you laughed as much as that, and then told me you didn't like it, I'd think you were an ungrateful old grump.'

'Promise I'm not that. First impressions notwithstanding.'

'That wasn't my first impression of you, Pete.'

'What was your first impression?' He paused, just before stepping into the aisle. There was no one behind them in this row, as the other couple further along had gone out the other end. 'Just out of interest…'

'Can't remember,' she answered him. 'When did we first meet?'

'Can't remember either. It wasn't when you came back from Sydney after you'd done your diploma in neonatal care?'

'Earlier than that, I think. I'm sure we came across each other before that. Much earlier. Years before.'

'I guess so. I've had visiting rights in the unit for close on seven years, although I stuck to very low-risk deliveries back then.'

'Then I know we did. We must have.'

'Remind me, then.'

'No, I can't.' She laughed. 'It's not a definite memory. But I've been there eight years, on and off.'

'There must be a moment,' he insisted, a smile touching his mouth and warming his eyes. 'A first moment.' He looked down at her, and his voice teased. 'I must have yelled at you…'

'I doubt it.'

'Or made you coffee.'

'It's nice that you do that. Lots of doctors don't.'

'Or discussed a news headline with you.'

'If so, it hasn't stuck.'

'No, it hasn't.' Pete smiled again. 'At some vague point, we just knew each other. No claps of thunder, or anything like that.'

'How unmemorable of us!'

'Maybe eventually we'll pin it down.'

'No, Pete, I think it's lost for all eternity in the mists of time.'

'Hypnosis might work.'

'Not on your life!'

Silly! Very silly! The credits had rolled through, and the cinema was empty but for themselves. They were just standing there, in the aisle, intrigued by how odd life was—that now, without admitting it in words, they could have become so important to each other, when there'd been no inkling of it for so many years before, nothing until her three months in Paris.

They should have kissed.

Before this.

Now.

Right at this moment, Pete should lean closer and sweetly touch her lips with his. He should say something soft and teasing about how it didn't matter if their first impressions hadn't been earth-shattering. Yes, they must have been blind before, but they weren't now, and they were together, and that was all that counted.

Emma could hardly breathe, and Pete hadn't moved. There were no more screenings in this cinema tonight, and a pair of cleaners had arrived. The still, breathless silence in the air should shatter into a thousand brilliant stars with a kiss, he should squeeze her close and they should float out of here together, leaving the cleaning team to its work. They would both know that they were going to stay together all night long.

But that would be so far beyond their boundaries and their unspoken rules that Emma didn't even know how to break the moment some other way, and continued to stand there, lost in the depths of his brown eyes.

'Ah, Emma,' Pete said at last. 'Ah, look! Let's go, before…'

He didn't finish, just stepped aside to let her go first, then followed her in silence. He walked her to her car, and she was painfully aware of him all the way, knowing he wouldn't kiss her when he said goodnight, hating herself for still hoping, despite everything, that he would.

Knowing Claire Croft only by sight, Emma was astonished to see her at her front door just two days later. Dressed in a flowing skirt and a close-fitting strappy top, she looked attractive and smart, and she'd parked her car in the driveway as if she were a frequent visitor.

Emma had a cold. It had descended on her the day after the movie and was still making her miserable. With a damp tissue pressed to her face, she invited Pete's wife—ex-wife?—to 'cub id', and thought immediately of Claire's friend, Mandy, whom she and Pete had run into at the cinema.

A report had obviously been made, and acted on.

'You've got a cold, poor thing,' Claire said, stepping forward into the front hall.

'Sorry, yes.' Emma led the way through to her small living room.

'Try lemon, garlic, ginger, honey and cayenne pepper in boiling water.'

'Uh, all right. I sometimes just drink hot lemon and honey.'

But Claire had finished with the subject of Emma's cold. 'You must know why I'm here,' she said.

'Not quite.' Emma paused, then added, 'And anyway, I'd rather hear it from you.'

'A friend saw you with Pete, and I made a few enquiries and found out who you were.'

'Yes, I wondered,' Emma murmured, but Claire didn't react.

'I'd been planning to cut short the Canberra visit anyway,' she said. 'Apparently, the two of you looked...' Suddenly, she was crying, and begging Emma, 'Don't, OK? I realise I have no right in the world to ask this of you. Pete will be free soon. And you're free already. But I need more time.'

'Claire, please, would you like some tea, or—?'

'No, no. I'm not staying.' She sniffed, took a tissue from the box on the coffee-table and pulled herself together again. 'The illness has been scary. You know about it...'

'A little.'

'I'm pretty sensible. I know this is likely to be for life, and I'm not going to get foolish and think I can keep in balance on my own. The medication is necessary, and it's making a huge difference. But it's scary to feel *flawed* like this.'

'It can happen to anyone, Claire. It's an illness as real and physical as flu or arthritis. You're not flawed.'

But Claire waved this reassurance aside. 'It's changed how I see my life. I do, seriously and simply, need the time. I'm not being catty. Pathetic, perhaps.' She smiled crookedly. 'But not catty. Pete and I haven't made a final decision about the girls, and I don't want him distracted by a new relationship and only too happy to park Jessie and Zoe with me so he can spend time with you.'

'I wouldn't want that either, Claire, and I'm sure Pete wouldn't let it happen, but in any case—'

'Thanks. *Thanks!*'

'Does Pete know you were coming to see me?'

'No! Heavens! This is between women and, look, there's really nothing more to say. I appreciate that you even let me in the door.'

'I really have no reason to feel badly towards you.'

'Some women wouldn't think so!' Claire moved in the direction of the front hall, and Emma took a handful of tissues and followed her, to watch her depart, whizzing her car rapidly backwards along the driveway thirty seconds later.

'Did I just agree that I wouldn't see Pete any more?' she murmured aloud. 'I don't think I did. Claire interpreted our conversation that way. But I didn't agree to anything.'

Should she have?

Surely not, when she and Pete hadn't even kissed. Still, she felt uncomfortable, as if Claire's whirlwind visit had shattered certain necessary and comfortable illusions.

CHAPTER EIGHT

EMMA liked the way the roster worked in the maternity department at Glenfallon Hospital.

Nursing staff were rotated in a loosely structured but regular triangle between Labour and Delivery, post-partum and clinic duties, which kept their skills honed in all aspects of a pregnant woman's care, from early prenatal visits through until the new mother went home with her baby.

This week, Emma was back in Labour and Delivery, and they were busy. It was the season for 'New Year babies'—all those conceived, with planning or by acci-dent, thanks to the relaxed atmosphere of the turning calendar nine months earlier.

Liz Stokes's baby didn't fall into that category—he was probably the result of the real-estate sales slump all through January!—but on Tuesday evening he an-nounced his intention of arriving with the New Year babies, regardless.

At thirty-eight and a half weeks, Liz was now per-mitted to get up to shower every day, and her labour began while she was standing beneath the hot water. Pete was called in at once, and after examining Liz he de-cided not to attempt to halt the labour. The baby was within the full-term range now, and he'd told Liz that he wanted to schedule her on Thursday in any case.

Liz remained in her room for a little longer, and was then wheeled across to Labour and Delivery and parked temporarily in the corridor leading to the obstetric operating theatre. She seemed pleased to see Emma there.

'I'm glad it's you.'

'You won't see very much of me,' Emma answered. 'You'll be under general anaesthesia.'

'Yes.' Liz frowned. 'I know that's what Dr Croft and I decided weeks ago. I was nervous about being awake, but...is it too late to change my mind?'

'I'm not sure,' Emma said. 'It's up to Dr Croft and the anaesthetist. And what about Warren? Is he going to be here?'

'He should be on his way in. That's one of the reasons I've changed my mind. I've been talking to a couple of other Caesarean mothers—I've met a few over the past couple of months!—and they've said how wonderful it was to be aware and clear-headed during their Caesareans, so that they could see the baby straight away. And Warren couldn't be there if I had a general, could he? He'd have to wait outside.'

'That's the rule, yes.'

'I think Warren would like to be there. We didn't plan this baby, we were very unsure at first, but now that he's almost here...' She got a little teary and shaky, and another contraction came, gripping her forcefully.

'Let me talk to the doctors,' Emma said.

The anaesthetist hadn't arrived yet, but Pete was at the nurses' station, talking to someone on the phone. His sister? Emma wondered. She heard him mention the girls. This was the first time she'd seen him since Claire's surprise visit yesterday. Her cold had dried up markedly, but her discomfort wasn't physical, it was mental.

Should she tell Pete about Claire, and what she'd said? Not now, obviously. The fact that she could legitimately put it off gave her a sense of reprieve that shamed her.

Instead, as soon as Pete had finished on the phone, Emma asked him what he thought about Liz's change of heart.

'I expect Clive will be OK with it,' he said. 'I'm OK with it, too, but I'll call in Gian instead of Alison, and I'll assist, instead of tackling it myself. With a conscious patient, I want this to go as smoothly as possible. Gian's had a lot more experience with complete placenta praevia than I have, and the ultrasound ten days ago confirmed that this one's going to be tricky.'

'You can say no, Pete, and insist on the general. Some doctors would.'

'Liz has had a rough time,' Pete answered. 'I'd like to give her this, since she wants it. It's a sign of how far she's come. She wasn't at all sure about this baby.'

'Yes, she just said something about that.'

'And she and Warren both pretended to themselves for a long time that he wasn't going to change their lives.'

'She'll be pleased.'

'Here's something I read when I was studying for my obstetrics diploma, Emma,' he said. 'A guy called Dr Tyler Smith said it in 1847, in a lecture that was published in *The Lancet*. He said that he hoped the day would come when "the lives of the mother and child shall never come into collision; when the painful thought of sacrificing or risking the one for the safety of the other shall never arise; and when there will be no difference between British or Continental, Catholic or Protestant action—the efforts of both being always exerted to save, and never to destroy." Don't you think that's nice?'

'You memorised it.'

'Because I thought it was so resonant. And what Smith wanted so much has happened. We're at that point now, in this country. At the time he was practising, Liz and her baby would probably both have died. As an outside chance, we might have saved one of them. Odds on the baby, not the mother. Today, our biggest choice is over which kind of anaesthetic to use.'

'You're giving me a chill down the spine, Pete.'

He grinned. 'Too frightening at this time of night?'

'No, too close to making me cry.'

'Never want to do that,' he said softly. 'Never, Emma.'

She looked at him, bathed in the heat of her awareness, but couldn't answer. Didn't want to tell him that he already had made her cry. She'd cried because of him last night. They'd had such a warm, comfortable evening, sitting beside each other at the cinema on Saturday, laughing in the dark. They'd come so close to a kiss, talking and teasing each other in the aisle while the credits had rolled. And then they'd parted on a couple of halting, awkward phrases beside her car.

Claire had shown up two days later with guns drawn, as if even such an innocent evening together was a betrayal and a threat.

That night, Emma had cried. For the mess. For her own foolishness. For the fact that Pete might need her in his life, but couldn't take what she most wanted to give.

Now, a day later, the evidence that he wanted to kiss her—and do much more than kiss her—was back, rich and simmering in the air like the smell of fresh-made chocolate. With Claire's entreaty, it seemed further from reality than ever.

Emma was glad there was no time to dwell on the moment. Liz's surgery took precedence.

With the higher than usual risk of a major bleed, due to the position of the placenta, Liz had given two units of her own blood several weeks earlier. This blood had been stored, and could be given back if necessary—an autologous blood transfusion, it was called.

After Emma had worked over her for a few minutes, Liz had a drip in the back of her hand and a catheter in place. Clive Anderson had arrived, and Gian Di Luzio was on his way.

'They're both OK about the epidural,' Pete told Emma as they scrubbed.

Warren Stokes stood beside his wife's wheeled bed, rocking back and forth on his heels and looking nervous. A contraction came, and Liz gripped his hand, panting and a little panicky. 'Hurry up!' she said. 'I'm scared. What if the baby starts pushing down? It's all blocked off down there, and he hasn't got anywhere to go.'

She was wheeled into the operating theatre a few moments later, and again she looked and sounded panicky. 'Maybe I should have had the general,' she said. 'How gory will this be?'

'Not at all, for you,' Pete reassured her. 'We'll put up a screen of surgical drapes. All you'll see is the baby, as soon as he's out and we can show him to you. Does he have a name yet?'

Dr Anderson had prepared the cannula for the epidural, and Emma knew Liz would shudder if she saw it. The question about a name provided a good distraction.

'Ben,' Liz said. 'We're going to call him Benjamin James.'

'Warren, can you sit here, right beside Liz's shoulder?'

'Liz,' said Clive, 'I'm going to get you to turn onto your side and curl up tight so your backbone is nice and clear for me.'

Dr Di Luzio entered unobtrusively. He threw a quick smile at Kit, then introduced himself to Liz. He and Pete nodded easily at each other, too. The two men were friends and got on well, Emma knew, which always made for a better atmosphere during surgery. She liked the sense of respect between them—part of Pete's essential nature, she was sure. He had an ability to inspire confidence and trust.

The drapes were set up as they waited for the anaesthesia to fully take hold.

'No more contractions!' Liz said on a breath of relief. 'This is amazing!'

'Can you feel this, Liz?' Clive asked.

'No. I can't feel anything.'

'This?'

'No.'

'That's good.'

The baby—Ben—was out in ten minutes, and he took a hearty breath and began to cry as soon as he felt the air on his skin and the light piercing into his eyes. Liz laughed and cried at the same time, and Warren just kept saying, 'Wow!'

The placenta was trickier than the baby. A syringe of oxytocin attached to Liz's drip line helped the uterus to contract, but the poorly positioned placenta wouldn't come away cleanly at first, and there was some heavy bleeding. If either Gian or Pete were concerned, they didn't let it show, speaking as easily and calmly as ever.

'We have blood, don't we?' Gian said briefly at one point.

'Two units,' Pete answered.

'Always good to know.' The obstetrician used the cautery to seal off a couple of stubborn vessels, and finally the placenta came away fully. During all this, Liz and Warren were too absorbed in their baby to realise that there was any drama, and it was soon over.

'That's nice now,' Gian commented, speaking of Liz's uterus. 'That's the way we want to see it, starting to tone up.'

'We'll have to take Ben away now, Liz,' Kit said.

'I'm not stitched up yet, am I?' she asked, frowning.

'No, that'll take another half an hour, and you'll see your baby in Recovery. You can even try him on the breast then, if you want to. Congratulations! He's perfect! Come on, little man...'

'It wasn't so bad. I'm glad I had the epidural. Oh, it all seems worth it now! All of it! He's so beautiful!'

'That was a good piece of work in the end, wasn't it?' Pete said.

'Are you still here?' Emma said blankly.

It was five past eleven, the night nurses had taken over and she'd come down the stairs to find Pete standing in the foyer of the building, scuffing his heels on the floor like a bored ten-year-old.

'By the time I was finished,' he said, 'It was almost eleven and I realised you'd be going off. Thought I might as well wait.' His gaze fell on her face briefly, then flicked away. 'See if you wanted coffee. I've never thanked you properly for all the work you did the other week, and I haven't said how much I enjoyed the movie with you on Saturday.'

'It was fun. The movie, and the garden.'

'That's not the point. You wouldn't do a garden for

anyone who asked, just because it was fun. You did it
for me, Emma, and you did it for other reasons.'

'Good ones,' she said awkwardly.

'I hope so. I don't know.' He looked down at her,
frowning. 'So, do you want coffee on your way home?
The girls are at Jackie's tonight.'

If there were good reasons to say no, Emma couldn't
remember what they were—not when Pete was looking
at her like that, not when she felt this way. They'd managed, until now, to keep within the boundaries they'd
wordlessly set for themselves. Why should tonight be
different?

'A quick one,' she said. 'And we can make it my
place, if you like. Can't really claim that your place is
on my way home.'

'I don't care where we go,' he answered. 'Or what we
do.'

As long as we're together.

He didn't say it, but it seemed so clear.

'Neither do I…' Emma's heart gave its usual giddy
lurch in her chest, and she wanted his company so badly
that she almost felt ill.

The hospital was so quiet at this time of night. Barring
emergencies that didn't impinge on this wing of the
building at the moment, visitors and most doctors had
gone home. The two of them were alone.

'My place, then,' she added shakily.

They left the building together and walked in the direction of the car park, not talking. Pete put his arm
around her, drawing her close to his side, and for a moment she let her head dip onto his shoulder, with her
chin tilted upwards a little, so that her forehead was
pressed against the warmth of his neck. If she'd lifted

her face just a little more, she could have pressed her lips to the same spot.

It felt too good. She lifted her head again and slid out of the circle of his arm. He let her go without protest, as if he hadn't wanted more. They both knew quite definitely, however, that he had.

He followed behind her car, through streets empty of traffic, and for some reason they both laughed when they got out of their cars in her driveway at the same time and met on her front path.

'Why is this funny?' he said.

'I don't know. It really isn't. Not at all.'

'It isn't,' he agreed. 'But we're laughing anyway.'

Just nerves, or something. Awareness. Stretched emotions, at breaking point and ready to snap.

They both sobered quickly, locked gazes and looked away again almost at once, as they so often did. Suddenly, Emma understood that tonight *was* different from all the other times they'd spent together.

Jessie and Zoe weren't here. There were no distractions, no safe havens to retreat to. There were no crowds of movie-goers around them, and she knew they weren't going to talk about gardens tonight.

'Come in, Pete,' she said, unlocking her front door and stepping inside. He followed her, shadowing her body closely. 'Coffee, wasn't it?' The hallway was dark, and she reached for a light that was too dim and too golden to drain the intimacy of night from the atmosphere.

'Whatever,' he said.

'Think I'm all out of whatever.'

'Then I'll just have what you're having.' They went down the corridor towards the kitchen, Emma leading the way.

She looked back at him and drawled, 'Nothing very rugged. Milo, made with hot milk. Are you game for that?' Her voice wobbled.

She moved to take the single step down to the sun-room, adjacent to the kitchen, but he reached out and held her arm, keeping her in place so he could step closer. 'Hey, are you OK?'

'A bit tense. Tired, I suppose. It's late.'

And Claire turned up here just yesterday, begging me not to do this.

'This was a mistake, wasn't it?' Pete said, almost as if she'd spoken aloud.

'I—I think so.'

She hadn't turned on any more lights, and the glow from the front hall barely reached this far. His face was shadowed as she looked up at him, but she could tell how intently he was watching her. Just the look in those brown eyes had the power to heat her to melting point.

'My fault,' he said. 'I wanted to talk. Claire is back.'

'I…uh…heard. I mean, I know.'

'I'm not letting her have the girls yet,' he ploughed on. 'I'm not sure why she didn't stay longer. She says she's fine now, and I know from her mother that she's taking her medication, but—'

'Can we please, please, not talk about Claire?' Emma begged desperately. 'I know we don't, very often…'

'No, we haven't.' He stiffened, and his eyes narrowed. 'I wouldn't have thought—'

'I'm sorry. I know. We hardly have at all. I know you need to. Perhaps more than we have. More than…I've let you, or something. I kept telling myself you wouldn't want to. That you'd want a break from thinking about it. I was protecting myself, not you, wasn't I? Kidding myself completely, I think.'

'Haven't noticed you doing very much of that,' he said softly, but she ignored him.

'And I know I'm a "friend". You should be able to talk to me about anything you like, trivial or important. But tonight I really, really don't want to talk about Claire.'

'Ah, you're right,' he rasped harshly. 'Oh, hell!'

'I think…perhaps…after all…you should just go.'

'No.' His eyes gleamed in the darkness. 'That's wrong. That's not what we need. You're right. Let's leave Claire out of it tonight. I want to talk about us, Emma. That's what we really need to talk about. It's time. It's way past time for this…'

He didn't talk, though. Didn't say anything more at all.

Instead, he brushed his knuckles against her neck, pushing her hair over her shoulder. He bent closer, his mouth steady and serious as he watched her lips, his face impossibly close now.

She pressed her lips together, then lapped her tongue between them, grazed her top teeth across her lower lip and waited, suddenly helpless, imprisoned by the hot depth of his eyes. She could see each silky lash, each agate-like segment of pattern in his golden brown irises.

His kiss came seconds later, and she'd wanted it for so long that it was impossible to turn her head away, impossible to do anything but sigh against him, wind her arms around him, feel him and want him even more powerfully than she'd wanted him all the times when they hadn't touched.

She loved him. Pointless to pretend any more. Pointless to reassure herself that she had any form of protection in place against her feelings, any limits, any boundaries. She loved him. It was all very simple. Or it could have been, in other circumstance.

The heat between them built like fire through dry wood, faster than the power of the mind to grasp. The touch of his mouth was urgent and full and he held her as if he would never be able to have enough of her, as if his desire for her had been surging towards this moment for weeks, and as if he was utterly certain that hers had, too.

He was right, of course. It had.

'Emma...' Pete's voice rasped in his throat. 'I knew it would be like this. I knew you'd feel like this.'

'Oh, Pete.' She almost sobbed his name, and pressed her mouth feverishly against his, hungry to taste him. She could already feel his arousal, hot and insistent, the wanted proof of his need.

'You knew it, too, didn't you?' he demanded.

'Yes.'

'Knew how much I wanted this...'

'Yes, of course I did. As much as I want it, too.' She was shaking, and could tell that he was as well. The muscles of his arms wrapped like iron bands around her, humming with tension.

'I kept kidding myself that it didn't have to happen,' he said, stealing sweet, swift, ravenous kisses from her at every word. 'And that if it didn't happen, we were OK. We weren't in trouble, or in danger, or doing the wrong thing.'

'So did I.'

'Tonight, to hell with all that, I just...don't...care...'

He deepened and steadied the pressure of his mouth, parted her lips and tasted her once more, held her hips then moved his hands upwards, claiming every part of her that he touched, branding her with sensations she knew would belong uniquely to her feelings for him forever.

'And I want more, Emma.'

'Yes. I know.'

'This is nowhere near enough.'

'No.'

They both tried to make it enough, however, straining against each other, pulling at clothes to gain access to living skin. His back was a warm sheet of muscle and bone, while the skin at his sides, below his arms, was supple and tender. His hands found the weight of her breasts and held them like coveted prizes through the fabric of her uniform. Her nipples tightened and jutted like cherry stones.

'I want to go to bed with you,' he said, his breath a hot flood against her neck, combing through her loosened hair. 'Tonight. Now.'

'Mmm…' Not yes, or no, just a sound of passion and need that he'd dragged out of her.

'I'm so tired of holding back on this, pretending we're friends, and that that's enough. It isn't. Friendship is so insipid when I feel like this and sense it in you. It isn't anywhere near enough, it hasn't been, ever since you came back from Paris, and I don't care about anything that might be in the way.'

And I care too much, she realised. *About him.*

Her heart was free, and it was virgin ground.

His wasn't. He couldn't love her. He wasn't free to. Not yet. Legally, morally, practically, he wasn't yet free.

And he might never be.

Only yesterday, his wife had come here to ask Emma not to let this happen.

'No…' she said feebly.

'Emma…it's so right. I want to show you…'

'No. Why are you doing this?' She spoke with her mouth still ravaging his between every word, and her arms still wrapped around him. He didn't even seem to hear. Hardly his fault, after the signals she'd sent out through every touch and every response. He found the zip at the back of her dress and slid it down.

The uniform dropped from her shoulders and fell in a pool around her feet. He cradled her breasts again, with only the lace of her bra as a barrier, then he dropped his hands to stroke the tops of her thighs, sending new tendrils of sensation coiling to her core.

Suddenly she was far too close to tears. She found the strength to pull away from him, wrapped her arms across her tingling breasts and forced steadiness into her voice, making it sound harsh.

'Why have you done this tonight of all nights?' she repeated. 'It's not fair! We managed not to for so long, and the fact that we hadn't…kissed…that we hadn't admitted to any of this, in words or in touch, was the only thing that made it possible. It isn't possible any more, Pete, now that we've started this. You're married.'

'Not for much longer.'

'I know things have been terrible with Claire lately, but your bed's hardly cold.'

'The final papers should be through in a few weeks. We separated a year ago. No, actually, it's longer. We tried again because of the girls—Claire wanted to—but it didn't work. And it's been over in our hearts even longer than it's been over on paper.'

'It *isn't* over. That's such a classic line. Pete, you need to know—'

'Are you suggesting I'm two-timing you in some way? Surely you can't be! Emma, I'm not!'

'No, that's not what I'm saying. I just believe—*feel*—

that a marriage isn't truly over until it's legally over, with everything decided. It's a moral issue. Partly. But it goes beyond that, too. You own a house together. You have two daughters. Have you worked out a property settlement? A custody arrangement?'

'No. With Claire's illness—'

'It matters, Pete. Those things aren't just details. Claire's illness isn't an excuse, it's a further impediment, and it's important. You can't know what you're going to feel about me when it's all settled.' She pressed her hands to her face. 'She came to see me yesterday.'

'She? Claire? Claire did? She only got back—'

'Yes, I know.' Emma reached down and dragged her uniform back up her body, struggling with the zip. Pete neither helped nor hindered her. 'The friend of hers who we ran into at the cinema...*alerted* her, I guess is the word.'

'What did she say?'

'She asked me not to let this happen. Said she wasn't being catty, just pathetic. She said she needed more time, and she didn't think it was fair to the girls to have you distracted by...well, this.'

'So you're in cahoots now, the two of you, both of you deciding on my behalf that it shouldn't happen.' His shoulders had stiffened even further. 'That's rich! Isn't it possible I could make that judgement for myself?'

'That's not— No, I don't mean it like that. Neither did she. I wish this hadn't happened! I wish I'd thought this through, seen it coming, and been stronger.'

'I don't.'

'Easy for you!' She threw the line at him, hardly thinking about its meaning, and he seized on it.

'Lord, do you think that's true?' He was very angry now. 'Really? That this is easy for me? In any way?

That I've done this lightly? That I held off at first, and then let this flare at last? I haven't done any of it lightly. I've thought about this.'

'With so much else to think about as well?'

'Yes! And I care about how you feel, Emma.' He hadn't said, I care about you, she noticed. Just 'I care about how you feel.' Crucial difference. She didn't blame him for it, it was simply a fact.

'Then help me!' she said. 'Can we possibly go back?'

'Pretend we never touched? Pretend we don't feel like this, and that we haven't talked about it, admitted to it? No, of course we can't! And I don't want to.'

'This is a refuge for you. You're still e-mailing me. If you tell me there's some substance behind this, some kind of promise, I won't believe you, because it can't be true. It can't! Not yet. Not with where your head and heart are placed right now. Not with Claire—how she is, and what she said. You've got so much still to work out, and to take care of.'

'Might it not help me to do that if you were around? Dear lord, don't I have the right to have anything for myself?' Pete's voice shook.

'I have been around!' she retorted. 'As a friend! That was the way to do this. That was the only way to make it work. To make the right space between the past and the future. You've made it impossible now!'

'You kissed me back, Emma,' he said quietly. 'Don't forget that. You very definitely kissed me back.'

She laughed, a twisted, complex little sound. 'Yes, I did. I'll take my share of blame for that, don't worry. It doesn't change anything. It just shatters our pretence even more thoroughly. We shouldn't have done this. And we shouldn't have pretended that friendship was innocent, and possible. It never was. Friendship was never on the cards!'

'Certainly seems like it isn't now,' he said. His voice was tight, and so was his face. She couldn't read him, couldn't gauge the depth of his anger, or its exact source. 'I should go,' he finished.

'That's all that's left, I think,' she agreed.

'I wanted to tell you about Claire coming back,' he said. 'Didn't realise you already knew. That's what I wanted to talk about, to tell you she and I might be able to push things through a little faster now. Decisions. Arrangements.'

'I hope it works out for you, Pete, and for her.'

'Most of all, for the girls.'

'Yes, of course.'

He stepped back. 'Was this the point we were always going to get to, no matter how we handled it, Emma? A realisation that the timing was completely wrong, and the ramifications too huge?'

'I don't know. I'm starting to think so.'

Pete nodded, but didn't speak, just began to walk towards the front door. When he reached it, he turned slightly. 'I'll see you.'

'Yes, I'm quite sure you will! More than either of us wants right now, perhaps!'

'No clap of thunder when we first met, and now there's no neat, clean goodbye.'

'It's—it's all right. We're reasonable people. We'll deal with it,' she said.

There was night-time, after all. Bed, with a pillow to cry into, and a back garden, with paths to pace restlessly on a moonlit night. He need never know about any of that.

'Goodnight, Emma,' he said, and opened the door.

She closed it for him seconds later.

CHAPTER NINE

CLAIRE looked good as she sat opposite Pete in the newly opened rear courtyard of the town's best restaurant-café, the Glenfallon Bakery. She had turned twenty-nine last week, and the twins celebrated their fifth birthdays this month as well. They were at preschool this morning.

She had had her hair freshly coloured, in the dark, golden-glinted shade that she favoured, and she was smartly casual in calf-length linen trousers and a pastel blue top with elbow-length sleeves. Her hair gleamed in the October sun as she sipped her cappuccino, and sunglasses shaded her eyes. She looked attractive, successful and in control, the way she'd been when she and Pete had first met.

With degree-level training in the hospitality and tourism industry, she'd come to Glenfallon six and a half years ago to work as Public Relations and Promotions Manager for Trevino Wines. She'd enjoyed the job, and she'd been good at it, with ambitions to rise higher. She'd envisaged promoting Australian wine and food internationally.

Her involvement with Pete and her pregnancy with the twins had derailed all of that. Pete could never for a moment wish his darling girls out of existence, but he knew that they hadn't been good for Claire. It was a problem he felt the two of them still hadn't solved.

So far, this morning, they'd had an amicable conversation, but Pete couldn't pretend to himself that he was fully relaxed. His goal for today was simple. If they could spend half an hour together over coffee without a major argument, he'd be happy. He knew they had a lot to work out, but that could wait.

If he'd felt any urgency in recent weeks, it was gone now, thanks to his blow-up with Emma the other night. She'd made it clear that he needed more than divorce papers in hand before he could embark on something new. He had the irrational sense that she'd callously abandoned him, although he knew she didn't see it that way. She'd hurt herself as much as she'd hurt him, taking the strong stance that she had.

'I've had some time to think, Pete,' Claire said. She nibbled a knuckle as she cleared her throat, betraying uncertainty beneath the polished veneer.

'You can have more,' he answered. He really didn't want her to come out with any rash, unworkable plans today. He'd grown so tired of those! He sensed she hadn't yet gone deep enough into what her problems were, and felt that her illness was almost irrelevant in some ways. Should he tell her that he knew about her pleading visit to Emma?

'No, I want to say it now,' she told him. She frowned and leaned forward. 'I think we should try again. Tear up the divorce papers and make a fresh start.'

Pete hid his appalled reaction.

'Didn't we already do that, and discover that it couldn't work?' he said, as calmly as he could. 'In fact, you were the first one to decide that it couldn't work.'

'That was before.'

Before her illness, he understood. He'd been afraid of this—that her illness would provide a convenient scapegoat for problems she must know, in her heart, had been there between them long before.

'Why are you saying this, Claire?'

She widened her eyes. 'Is it that easy for you to give up on our marriage?'

Easy?

'We had good reasons for doing so, more than a year ago,' he answered. 'This state of limbo has already dragged on for far too long. I wasn't— My question wasn't a challenge, Claire. I just think you need to ask yourself why you're so sure it would be a good idea. What's motivating you? It isn't love.'

Would she concede that? He waited, and watched her regain her ground quickly.

'No,' she agreed, 'but I respect you, Pete. I admire you. As a person.'

'And it isn't because it would be better for the girls.' He continued his argument doggedly, although he didn't have much faith that she'd genuinely listen. 'If we can work out a sensible custody arrangement, they'll have a steadier life with much less conflict. I don't want them getting caught up in the mess we've made. I don't want them hurt and confused and insecure.'

'No. Of course. Neither do I.' She shifted in her seat and reached for her coffee again.

She'd tensed at the phrase 'sensible custody arrangement' as if it frightened her. He didn't know why. He'd withdrawn his petition for sole custody, on the understanding that Claire was genuinely committed to keeping her illness under control with medication. Her mother had come to Glenfallon with her, too, and fifty-three-year-old Hester was a strong and sensible woman.

Pete had no qualms about leaving the girls in Claire's care when their grandmother was around, but he hated the fact that, yet again, Jessie and Zoe would have to adjust to a new routine.

'I'm just not ready to close off our options,' Claire said.

Pete's stomach felt like a stone. The organ had been like this—heavy and churning, robbing him of appetite—since the night of Liz Stokes's Caesarean last Tuesday, when he and Emma had let their feelings for each other spill so disastrously into the open.

He hadn't seen her since, apart from one or two stray glimpses around the hospital, and he was angry every time he thought about what she'd said—and that was almost constantly.

Even given Claire's entreaty to her, how could she take such a hard line? he'd asked himself. The two of them had known each other for years as colleagues, and lately as friends. Was she running away purely because she didn't want to have to deal with problems and complexities? She wasn't a coward in that way, surely!

This was how his thinking had run all week.

Now, for the first time, he wondered if she might have been right, if that brief visit from Claire had given her a more accurate insight than he possessed.

'No,' he answered Claire. 'We have to close off options.' He managed to keep his voice calm. 'This is what's worst for the girls. The uncertainty. The chopping and changing. The makeshift arrangements that don't hold together. The sense that everything's still possible, so nothing's ever actually going to happen.'

But as usual Claire hardly seemed to hear, and she looked frightened. So much for his plan to keep this easy and light and safe today! So much for his sense that she needed time. Now he was pushing her.

'Why did you stay such a short time in Canberra?' he asked her. 'Were you bored?'

At this, she brightened. 'No, not at all. Mum's very

good at keeping me busy! We got on really well.' She smiled. 'Like sisters. She's been wonderful. She thinks I should do a course next year. Update my qualifications or move into another area. Graphic design is a possibility. Or a higher business degree. I could see myself managing a hotel or a function centre.'

'Then why don't you?'

'I can't abandon you. I—The girls—I—' The panicky look appeared on her face again. 'I had to come back. I'm their mother.'

'And no one's ever going to take that away from you, Claire.' He kept his voice to the calm, soothing pitch that seemed appropriate. 'You need to be fully stable with your medication before we talk about how we're going to balance their care. If you did go and live with your mother, we'd work that out, too. Somehow,' he added bleakly, wondering how he'd deal with only seeing his daughters something like one weekend a month.

I need to talk to Emma, he realised. He needed to apologise.

He'd been as wilfully blind as Claire in many ways. He'd been so sure about the building strength in what he felt for Emma, but how much of it had been, as she'd suggested, about his desperate need for an escape? How perceptive could he be at the moment about his own feelings and his own future?

He couldn't trust either his certainty or his pain.

People often went through a transitional relationship after surviving a divorce, but Emma deserved far better than to be his temporary therapy or his vacation from real life. He wouldn't hurt her any more than he already had, and they both needed to be clear on that.

Talking to her was quite simple, as it turned out. He limped through another ten minutes with Claire, and at least she agreed to proceed with the divorce. He urged her to think again about what she really wanted, then headed for the hospital to take his turn at the weekly prenatal clinic.

Here, pregnant patients under the primary care of the hospital midwives were given an extra check-up by a doctor at certain points in their pregnancy to make sure that any unusual problems were caught. He discovered as soon as he arrived that Emma was rostered as the assisting nurse today, and took his opportunity at once.

'I'm sorry, Emma, about the other night.'

Emma froze as soon as she heard his voice, then looked up slowly. She sat at the desk where the morning's patients would come to check in, with a pile of files in front of her. There were already two women waiting and a couple of children playing noisily with toys in the corner.

She hadn't heard Pete's approach across the carpeted floor. He'd reached her before speaking, in a low tone that only she would hear. Now his eyes were fixed on her face, their warm brown depths smouldering like unseasoned wood.

'Pete.' His name escaped her lips like a bubble floating upwards in water. She didn't know what else to say.

'You were right in what you said,' he went on. 'I pulled you into my life at the wrong time. For both of us. I wasn't thinking clearly, and I was out of line. I hope you can forgive the clumsiness, and the blindness—of the way it started, and the way it finished.'

'Yes,' she answered awkwardly, afraid of being overheard. 'Of course I can. I understand the reasons.'

'And that you can get on with your life.'

'That's harder,' she blurted out, too churned up to be anything but honest.

He gave her a suffering look. 'Actually, you *shouldn't* forgive me,' he said.

'I told you I did. You just asked me to.'

'That was shallow. And unreasonable. One day perhaps I'll forgive myself.' With patients waiting, there wasn't any more they could say. For the best, probably. They'd only be going around in circles. Emma was about to hand him the first patient file, but then he added in a different tone, 'I had a call from Alethea Childer's cardiologist in Melbourne, by the way.'

'Oh, yes?'

'Not the best news. She has an infection. The kind of setback she didn't need when they were hoping to proceed with her second surgery soon.'

'No, she didn't need anything like that! That's so disappointing!' Emma blinked back tears. Already vulnerable to emotion, the news about tiny Alethea cast her spirits down still further.

'So far, she's fighting it,' Pete said, 'but, of course it'll delay her discharge, and it's tough on Rebecca and her mother.'

'They're both still there?'

'Yes, and planning to stay as long as it takes. I've told them I want to see that baby the day she gets home!'

'Me, too,' Emma agreed, hardly aware of what she was saying. Her throat was still tight. Any second her eyes would brim over, and what would the waiting maternity patients think? She couldn't give way to her feelings now! 'She was a darling, those few days we had her. A real fighter.'

'She still needs to be.' They looked at each other in awkward silence for a moment, then he cleared his throat. 'Do you have a file there for me? We're running a bit late now.'

'Yes, um, OK, your first patient is Mrs Gouzvaris, whose glucose tolerance test result came back too high yesterday,' Emma said quickly. 'Here's the file, and she's waiting. Her English isn't great.'

'Thanks.' He looked at the waiting patients, and correctly guessed which was the one he wanted—an attractive dark-haired woman with a few threads of silver in her hair, Emma had noticed. 'Mrs Gouzvaris? Come through, will you?' he said.

Emma struggled through the rest of the clinic and was painfully relieved when it was over. A week went by, in which she only saw Pete a couple of times at a distance. Kit and Gian had set a definite date for their wedding now, not the Saturday they'd asked their friends to pencil in but a Friday evening several weeks later, in early December. They would then fly to Sydney for a long-weekend honeymoon.

Emma received her invitation in the mail when she got home from work on a Thursday afternoon. 'Emma and guest,' it said. But there was no one she wanted to bring. Only Pete. She didn't seriously consider asking him, and realised almost at once that in any case he'd be bound to receive an invitation of his own. He and Gian were good friends.

Although the wedding was still weeks away, she dreaded the idea of seeing Pete in such a setting. She'd already promised Kit that she would wear her Paris dress, and even if she didn't, if she wore some dowdy sack in an unflattering colour, weddings were…impossible occasions, really, when you were alone and not happy about it.

In telling Pete that they couldn't deepen their involvement with each other until and unless he'd sorted out the unresolved issues between himself and Claire, had

Emma drawn too firm a line in the sand? She didn't
know the exact date on which Pete would be legally free,
but it must be soon.

She began to hope that he would phone the moment
it happened. That he'd zoom round to her house in the
open-topped red Ferrari she and Nell had joked about
weeks ago, with the divorce papers fluttering in his hand,
when she just happened to be perfectly dressed. Add a
bouquet of crimson roses. Sunset. Violins. Pete would
whirl her into his arms and—

Ugh. Hopeless.

Emma laughed at herself over the fantasy, and did her
best to put it aside.

'Well, if it had been me, I would have gone to Sydney
for a wedding dress,' Caroline told Kit. 'But you've
proved it's not necessary. You look just gorgeous!'

Caroline clasped her hands over her heart as she
spoke. She had pink cheeks and sparkling eyes and a
dreamy, far-away smile on her face, which made it clear
that Emma wasn't the only one who ever had romantic
fantasies and wistful hopes. Caroline hadn't been jaded
by her long-ago divorce. She'd defiantly become more
of a romantic than ever.

'Yes, it's perfect, Kit,' Emma agreed.

Even cynical Nell drawled, 'You'll do, girl. If I cry
at the wedding, you know I'm going to hold you personally responsible. I hate it when I cry at weddings!'

'And you always do, Nell,' Caroline pointed out
cheerfully.

'Thanks for reminding me!'

'But does it fit right?'

Kit craned and twisted in front of the long mirror in
the master bedroom at her fiancé's family farmhouse.

The place was in a state of upheaval at the moment as Gian and Kit's possessions had just been moved in and Federica Di Luzio's had been moved out, to her son's two-bedroom unit in town. The wedding was only a week away.

'It fits as if it grew on you,' Caroline said.

'Mrs Seccomb said if it felt too tight around the waist she'd let it out. I don't know if that was a hint.'

'Oh, *are* you, Kit?' Caroline shrieked. 'Pregnant? That's—!'

'No. *No.*' Kit flushed darkly at once, and she looked very uncomfortable. 'That's not what I meant. A hint that I was getting chunky. And Federica has been teaching me all these wonderful Italian recipes, so—'

'Trust me, Kit,' Caroline said, 'if it *was* a hint, it was about a very particular kind of weight gain. I know June Seccomb. She *always* assumes brides are pregnant and makes sure they know that it's never too late to let out the dress. Now, are you *sure*?' Caroline wore a cajoling smile.

She meant it as a tease, Emma could see, but Kit cut her off at once, far too quietly.

'Stop, Caroline,' she said. 'Don't, please. It's probably time I told you this. Told all of you.' There was a sudden silence, and a change of atmosphere in the cool bedroom. 'It's unlikely that Gian and I will be able to have a child of our own. So…I know it's kindly meant, Caroline, but, please, don't tease about it. I—I had a long struggle with infertility in a previous relationship, before Gian and I even met, and we're going to have to look at IVF and other forms of assisted reproduction to even give ourselves a chance.'

Caroline hid her face in her hands for a moment, then

raised her head again. 'Lord, I'm so clumsy!' she whispered. 'I'm so sorry, Kit, I had no idea!'

'Why should you? I don't tell people very much. Gian's known for months. It was a problem for a while.'

'For Gian?' Nell said, frowning.

'No, for me. I couldn't believe, for a long time, that it wouldn't destroy our relationship. It destroyed my last one. But Gian is different.' She smiled. 'And I realised that in the end.'

'I don't want to sound crass,' Nell said. 'But you'll have Bonnie, too.'

'No,' Kit said firmly. 'She's not a substitute. She's *herself*. I was telling Gian that—yelling it, actually—when it all clicked into place for me. If Bonnie is just Bonnie, and Gian is just Gian, then I couldn't encumber him with James's blind spots and weaknesses.'

'No, of course not,' Nell agreed quietly. 'He's a good man.'

'If we loved each other, which is…uh…a given at this stage, but it wasn't a few months ago, then I had to credit him with the ability to behave differently to James. Anyway, that's the story, and I'm glad you all know. OK, now I'm going to be like Emma when she first got back from Paris.' Kit grinned. 'Can we get back to what's really on my mind? The dress?'

'It's not too tight, Kit,' Emma said. 'It really is perfect.'

Perfect, she thought later on alone at home, even though Kit's life wasn't. She had a man whom she loved and was about to marry, she had a beautiful home to make her own, and she had a gorgeous little adopted daughter.

And I've been assuming that her life was perfect, Emma realised. She'd even had some moments of raw, miserable envy which she'd been ashamed of at the time, and was even more ashamed of now. But it's not perfect. Which only goes to show…

What? She wasn't quite sure. That you could look as radiantly happy as Kit and Gian did, even when life sent you lemons? That problems could sometimes be accepted even if they couldn't be overcome?

She guessed that she and Kit and Nell and Caroline wouldn't talk again about Kit's infertility. Kit had given out some pretty strong signals that she wouldn't want to. But Emma suspected that Kit's revelation this afternoon had brought all four of them closer in some way, and given them each something different to think about.

Nell hadn't said much after Kit had put the dress away and made them all a pot of tea. Caroline had announced, 'I want to phone Josh, make sure he's OK by himself at home, and tell him I'll be there soon.' Kit's revelation had probably reminded Caroline of the precious legacy of her failed marriage. She always spoke so proudly of her son.

'He's going to be my "and guest", Kit,' she'd said today. 'Did you notice on our RSVP?'

'Yes, I've put his name on our list.'

'And he's even going to dance with me. Mind you, he initially wanted a dollar a minute to do it, but he dropped his price in the end!'

How did Kit's revelation reflect on me? Emma wondered. Thinking about it for a few minutes, she realised it had given her some courage, and some hope, albeit a faint one, that she and Pete still had a chance.

'I was hoping we'd have a baby on my shift,' Mary Ellen Leigh told Emma at the hand-over the following afternoon. 'Janelle was doing so well at first, but the contractions have eased off since she stopped walking around. It'll be another couple of hours, I should think. But so far it's all routine for a first baby. Head down, at zero station, occiput anterior position, good strong heartbeat. The cervix is fully effaced and dilated to around five or six centimetres as of fifteen minutes ago.'

She detailed more information about the patient's current condition and prior history, all of it straightforward.

'Thanks, Mary Ellen,' Emma said when she'd heard everything.

'They're a nice couple. She's been seeing Pete Croft through the pregnancy, and wants him at the birth if possible. I'd say she'll be delaying his dinner.'

Pete! Emma hadn't come across one of his patients in here for a while.

She opened her mouth to say something about his girls. It was their dinner she'd worry about. Pete could handle a rumbling stomach. But his childcare arrangements weren't her concern, and in any case she didn't want her fellow midwives speculating about the nature of their relationship.

As far as she knew, no one suspected that they'd almost trespassed into an involvement a month or two ago. This made her current turmoil and uncertainty a little easier to take. She didn't have to field awkward questions or mistaken assumptions.

'Enjoy your weekend,' she told her departing colleague, and went in to see her new patient.

Janelle Hancock was in her early thirties, and worked at a pharmacy in the centre of town. She and her husband were committed to an intervention-free birth, and had good odds of achieving their goal. Chris Hancock finished timing a contraction and told Emma, 'Down to six minutes apart. They were two minutes apart earlier. What's going on?'

'They'll probably pick up again if you could walk around some more, Janelle. You're obviously getting a bit too comfortable here on the bed!'

'Ha! Comfortable?' Janelle sniffed and laughed and groaned.

'Could you try it for a bit? If it doesn't feel good, we can do something else. A shower?'

'We haven't tried a shower yet,' Chris said.

'OK, a walk and a shower,' Emma coaxed. 'Nice if we could get you to your room and settled with the baby by dinnertime. You'll be hungry then.'

'I don't believe that, but all right.'

Emma and Chris helped her up, and she did several laps of the corridor. The contractions picked up rapidly, and by the time she got back to the shower, she was ready for its relaxing effect.

'This is the worst one yet,' she gasped.

Emma got the water running to the right temperature, then left Janelle and Chris alone for a few minutes. Janelle let the hot water run over her back and abdomen, while Chris got half-drenched holding her up and giving her a rub. Out at the nurses' station, Emma phoned Pete. He'd been told earlier in the day that Janelle's labour had begun, so she knew he'd be prepared.

'Not long now,' she told him, finding it hard to maintain the right balance between professionalism and warmth. 'You'd better come in.'

'On my way,' he answered.

'We'll see you, then.' She wanted to ask him about the girls. Were they with him, or with Claire? Would it matter if this birth took an unexpected turn and he had to spend longer here than he'd planned?

But it wasn't her problem.

It could have been. She might have been fully caught up in his life by now, if she hadn't said no to him the night of Liz Stokes's delivery.

Or she might have pulled both of them into an even bigger and more painful mess of regret.

'I really don't like this!' Janelle's moan spilled from her room as Emma returned to her. 'I can't get comfortable. Don't just stand there, Chris. Oh, here it comes again.' She heaved lungfuls of air in and out with desperate force, trying to ease pain too severe to talk through. At last the contraction ebbed, but another one began to build almost immediately, and she moaned again. 'Oh, it's not stopping…'

She was leaning over the bed, with Chris massaging her shoulders ineffectually. Poor man, it wasn't his fault that he couldn't be of much use. Janelle had gone into transitional-stage labour, when the last few centimetres of dilatation took place much more rapidly, and each contraction shoved the baby's head deeper into the tight girdle of the pelvis.

Pete would get here only just in time.

'Something's happening,' Janelle gasped a few minutes later. 'I think I need… I can't stand up.'

'Do you need to push?' Emma asked. 'Are you feeling pressure?'

'Yes…No… I just need to get comfortable.'

She'd begun to panic and sweat. Emma tried to read the language of her restless body. Which position to suggest? She obviously wasn't comfortable on her feet. Some women ended up squatting, or kneeling on the bed on all fours. Many still preferred the traditional position that doctors had dictated in the past—on their backs, with legs drawn up and pressed open.

Janelle leaned on the bed again, just as Pete came through the door. He took in the situation at a glance, and realised she was very close to delivery.

'Like this?' he muttered to Emma.

'I haven't suggested anything yet,' she answered. 'She says she's not comfortable, but…' She stopped.

Janelle had begun to strain with all her might, leaning head and chest and forearms on the bed. Chris was beside her, trying to support her and whispering words of encouragement.

'Think it's going to be like this,' Pete said. 'Janelle, can you reach down and tell me if you can feel the baby?' he asked.

'No.'

'Try for me. Just have a go. Nothing lost if you can't manage it. Let's see if it's crowning. I think we're nearly there.'

'OK, I'll try.' The contraction eased, giving her more confidence. Her hand was clumsy and groping, but she managed a smile after a few moments. 'Yes, I can feel it! I can feel it!'

Another contraction came and she pushed again, dissipating too much of her energy in groaning. Emma came in close to help Chris hold her, and coached, 'Down, Janelle. Push down. Don't let it come up through your throat. You're doing great. The baby's almost here.'

'Fantastic, Janelle,' Pete said. 'We'll have the head on the next contraction.'

He had to take an awkward position himself to catch the baby.

'Legs further apart if you can, Janelle,' Emma said. 'Chris, if you could support her lower down?'

Janelle pushed again, more efficiently this time, and

the head squeezed free. Pete checked that the cord was clear and rotated the shoulders. Janelle panted desperately, and as soon as the next contraction began she gave another push and a little boy was fully born. He cried at once and fought Pete's attempts to suction out his nose and throat.

The new parents were both in tears. Emma clamped the cord as Janelle slumped forward onto the bed. 'Oh, a boy!' she said. 'A beautiful boy! This is amazing!'

'You've done really well, Janelle,' Pete told her. 'Would you like us to help you onto the bed, now, and you can hold him?'

For the next ten minutes, Janelle and Chris were oblivious to everything but baby Lachlan, while Pete waited for a final spate of mild contractions and delivered an intact and good-sized placenta, which Emma took for weighing.

'Tiny tear,' Pete said to her quietly. 'I'm not even going to stitch it, because in that position, it'll heal better on its own.'

'You won't be late for dinner after all,' Emma commented.

'Dinner?'

'Oh, nothing. Mary Ellen thought Janelle might go slower than this and you'd miss your meal, that's all.'

Pete didn't answer for a moment, but Emma felt his eyes upon her, making her heat up as if she were under a barrage of operating lights. 'I guess you're eating at the hospital,' he finally said.

'I only came on at three,' she answered. 'I'll grab a break once mum and bub are settled in post-partum.'

'I'd...uh... I mean, I often grab something in the cafeteria, but tonight I have to pick up the girls.'

'Right.' She hesitated, then asked before she could

rethink the wisdom of the question, 'How's it all going, Pete?'

'Taking its time. Limping along. Claire is going to put the house on the market. She definitely wants to study in Canberra next year. I can't stand in the way. It'll be too good for her mental and emotional health for me to block the idea.'

'But it won't be good for yours.'

'She's planning to take the girls so, no, it won't be good for mine.' He tried to smile, but failed miserably. 'I don't want them to go. If the move to Canberra looks permanent, I'll probably look at selling up and relocating there myself. So much for our garden!'

Emma touched his sleeve. Such an inadequate gesture of support, but it was all she could give, and any sense that the time might soon be right for a second chance between them evaporated like morning mist.

CHAPTER TEN

GIAN DI LUZIO and Kit McConnell were getting married this afternoon. Pete had cleared his schedule as far as possible, but there was always the danger of running behind and finishing late.

His senior receptionist, Angela Meredith, had already presented him with a couple of patients she thought he would want to squeeze in, and she'd been right. Angela had good diagnostic instincts. He saw one of the squeeze-ins and sent the man straight off to hospital with suspected heart trouble, then had to spend longer than scheduled on another patient, whom he'd wrongly anticipated would be routine.

The waiting room looked more crowded every time he went out to pick up his next file. Then came a few easy cases. The three-year-old with the rash didn't have impetigo. Forty-five-year-old Sarah Lessing's mole did look nasty, but only because it had got scratched recently. It didn't need a biopsy. Next, a middle trimester prenatal visit took just a few minutes.

The waiting room didn't look so frightening any more. Then Angela's alert diagnostic instincts came into play once again and she intercepted him, with her hand held over the mouthpiece of the phone, before he called in his next patient.

'Claire,' was all she said, in the carefully neutral undertone she always used for his ex-wife now.

Claire often phoned him at the surgery, and almost always on the subject of the girls, but she usually picked her moments better than this. She usually needed time to talk, too, or she wanted to get out of a prearranged interval with the girls.

'I can't take them this weekend after all,' the story would go. 'Can they stay on with you? Mum's got a gastric upset, and the real-estate agent has scheduled three sets of people to come through the house.'

She'd put their marital home on the market and applied for a full-time course in Canberra. He hadn't come to terms with this last reality yet—that Jessie and Zoe would be living four hours' drive away in just a few months' time. Instead, he had put off any concrete plan for a move of his own, and always agreed at once to any proposed change of plan for the day, only too glad to spend more precious hours with his daughters and avoid yet another packing of their well-travelled overnight bags.

This phone call today, when he had a good friend's wedding to attend a few hours from now, was one of the few occasions when he wouldn't welcome taking the girls.

'I'll take it inside,' he told Angela, and she nodded and switched the call through to the phone in his office.

'Help, Pete!' Claire squealed into the phone as soon as he spoke her name. 'Zoe fell off the climbing set and she's done something to her arm.'

'Broken?'

'I—I don't know. She's just holding it against her body and crying. She won't show me. I think it must be, but I can't see, and I'm all shaky.'

'Can you drive?'

'Yes. Yes, I can do that.' She took a deep breath. 'I have to calm down a bit, don't I?'

'Bring her in, and I'll take a look.'

'It was all my fault. I wasn't—'

'Don't think about that now. Just get here as soon as you can.' He looked at his watch. A quarter to four. If she hadn't got around to making Jessie and Zoe an afternoon snack yet, and that was likely… 'Grab a couple of muesli bars for them, Claire.'

'I don't think I have any.'

'Something, then. Something quick. Cheese sticks? Banana? Cake?'

'I— OK. Yes. There must be something.'

'Something quick,' he repeated, then could feel her getting frazzled down the phone. She didn't think ahead, and then panicked at small, practical suggestions like this. He shouldn't have said anything. He almost barked at her, Forget it! But he didn't want her to feel inadequate, so he told her more gently instead, 'If you don't have anything to hand, don't worry. Just come straight in.'

He fitted in two more patients between ending the call and seeing Claire and the girls walk through the door. Jessie had a big bag of corn chips in her hand, and was feeding the odd one to Zoe, in between swallowing handfuls of them herself. Zoe obviously felt too miserable to be hungry.

As Claire had said, she cradled her arm against her body like an injured animal, and still had tears of pain running down her face. Pretty convinced that the arm was indeed broken, Pete took all three of them straight into his office.

'Now, where does it hurt, darling?' he asked.

He expected her to point to an area between wrist and elbow, where most children's arm fractures occurred, but instead she touched her shoulder. 'Up the top,' she said.

The humerus? An unusual break. It would need the

confirmation of an X-ray, but even if it was broken, this particular kind of fracture couldn't be put in a cast, short of encasing Zoe's entire shoulder and half her chest in plaster.

A broken humerus could be an indication of non-accidental injury. He didn't suspect that in this case, and wouldn't have believed it without absolute proof, but he had to ask. 'How exactly did it happen, Zoe?'

'I was playing on the climbing set.'

'In the garden at Mummy's?' He knew Claire's answer to this already, of course.

'Yes.' Zoe nodded. 'And my foot got caught when I jumped down, and I was hanging, then I fell on my arm.'

He felt a wash of relief that he fought to keep from showing. He *hadn't* suspected Claire. She could be vague and diffident and disorganised with the children, yes, but never cruel or hot-tempered. All the same, Zoe's convincingly clear-eyed and simple account, so different from the coached and rehearsed stories he'd heard from frightened abused children a couple of times in his career, took away a terrible, illogical fear.

'It's all my fault,' Claire said.

He touched her arm. 'I'm sure it wasn't.'

'I was inside the house, talking on the phone. I wasn't watching them.'

'You can't sit and stare at them constantly while they play, at their age. The garden's safe from any obvious dangers. This was just one of those things. You'll have to take her up to the radiology clinic across from the hospital for an X-ray, but I'm going to go with what I suspect and put it in a sling now. That'll ease the pain, and I'll give her some paracetamol as well.'

He looked at Claire. She was shaky and pale.

'Angela will make you some tea. Jess, do you want

to watch me make a sling for Zoe's arm, or will you go
and play toys in the waiting room?'

'Play toys,' Jessie said.

'I'll sit with her,' Claire said promptly. She just didn't
function well in this kind of situation.

Zoe had stopped crying. 'Is it not hurting so much
now?' he asked her.

'Not so much,' she answered.

'That's because you're holding it nice and still, and
the sling and the medicine will help, too.'

'Will I have to have an injection?'

'No, sweetheart, and the X-ray won't hurt either.'

He drew up a dose of liquid paracetamol in a plastic
syringe and Zoe sat obediently still while he squirted it
into her mouth. It had a strawberry flavour, and most
children liked it enough to refrain from fighting and spit-
ting it out.

He buzzed through to Angela, and asked her to make
Claire some tea, with milk and sugar, then folded a big
square of gauze into a firm sling and gave Zoe an orange
lollipop from the secret stash of bravery awards in his
desk, kept for just such occasions as this.

He sent her out to lick it in the waiting room, while
she watched her sister play. She had become much more
cheerful already.

Meanwhile, Angela had her hand over the mouthpiece
of the phone again, and that this-is-a-call-you'll-want-to-
hear-about look on her face.

All right, what now? The waiting room had begun to
resemble a peak-hour city train station again.

'Hit me with it, Angela,' he said. 'What emergency is
this?'

'No, you'll like this one,' she answered. 'It's Rebecca

Childer. Alethea is home from Royal Children's, and doing well.'

'That's great!'

'Rebecca is wondering if you'd like to see the baby this afternoon if she brings her in. Apparently you'd told her ages ago that you wanted to see her as soon as they got back. She sounds...' Angela searched for the right word '...keen.'

'Does she?' He caught his receptionist's sub-text. *Don't say no.* 'Tell her, yes, I'd love to see Alethea.'

Only I'd rather it wasn't this afternoon.

Angela smiled, satisfied. Just who was in charge here, anyway? Pete wondered briefly.

'Claire, can we talk?' he said to his ex-wife, and she must have read an ominous meaning into his words which he hadn't intended, because her face went tight and her nod was a jerk of tension, as if she were a puppet and an unseen hand had just pulled a string.

When the two of them were shut in his office, he tried to stay positive and reassuring, but he had that crowded waiting room out there, and Rebecca on her way in with her fragile little heroine. He just didn't have a lot of time for this.

'Now, they'll have to take the sling off again for the X-ray, of course,' he said. 'I've written out the form, and booked her in. Four-fifteen, which is...' he looked at his watch again '...soon. But at this time of day, they're probably running a bit late.'

Aren't we all?

'They'll help you put the sling back on,' he continued, 'but you may have trouble with it over the next few days. Kids can't keep still. It'll work loose, or something. You can buy shaped slings at the pharmacy, and I'd suggest doing that today, because you're bound to need it. You can also pick up some over-the-counter pain medicine that's a little stronger than what you'd have at home. Talk to the pharmacist.'

Nothing too onerous in any of that, he thought, and looked at her, waiting for a nod, or a question, or—

'I can't do this, Pete,' she said.

'Yes, you can,' he coached her patiently. 'She's stopped crying. She's OK.'

'No. I mean all of it.' She waved her hands. 'I'm not good with them. I never was. I'm supposed to be, because mothers just *are*, and I've been trying. I kept thinking if we could sort out our marriage, at least you were around, too, but we couldn't manage that in the end and— Today seems like the last straw. I hate this! How terrible would it be if I don't take them to Canberra with me when I move? If I left them here with you?'

Her face was tight, pleading for reassurance and agreement. Her hands were screwed up so tight that her nails had to be gouging into her palms, and her knuckles were white. It had cost her so much to say this, and to understand her own feelings in the first place.

How terrible would it be?

A sudden crystal clear light flooded the whole landscape of Pete's life. His marriage. Claire. The girls. His agonised sense, lately, that he ought to move to Canberra, too. His failed attempt at a relationship with Emma, which still ate at him every time they met.

And he thought, *Of course!* Is this why it's been so hard for Claire to come up with a consistent plan? It is! This has been a huge part of the problem all along! She'd been impossibly torn between what she thought she should feel, and what she really did feel, and she hadn't been able to admit it, even to herself.

'It wouldn't be terrible, Claire,' he answered, his

voice rough with urgent sincerity. 'It's probably the best decision you could make, the absolute best, and a courageous one, too.'

'I want to see them, have them for holiday visits, phone them and send them presents and put their paintings on my fridge and boast about them to my friends and *all* of that,' she answered, fast and shaky, as if she still had to convince him. 'But I just can't have them. I panic. I do it wrong. I'm not good for them, and they're not good for me in the long run. They need to live here, with you.' She blinked tears from her eyes.

'We'll talk about it some more when I've finished for the day,' he told her gently. Mentally, he waved goodbye to Gian's and Kit's wedding, doubting he'd get there at all. 'We'll meet at your house and give them an early meal in front of a video while we get the practical stuff sorted out. I think this is the best decision you've made, Claire, and I support it fully.'

'I just couldn't admit it to myself.'

'Because mothers aren't supposed to feel that way. Mothers cop too much flak!'

'Half the time from themselves!'

'Things are going to seem clearer for both of us now.'

'Tell me again about what I have to ask for at the pharmacy. Write it down.'

'No, tell you what, I'll phone Trevor White—you know, the pharmacy in Hill Street, on the way to your place—and he'll have the right sling and the right medicine ready for you when you get there.'

'Thanks, Pete. Thanks for everything.'

Claire and the girls left for the radiology clinic. Pete saw another patient, and then a series of cooing exclamations just beyond his office door told him that

Rebecca and her baby had arrived. He went out, and the first person he saw in his waiting room was Emma.

She hadn't caught sight of him yet, because she was too busy cooing at the baby in Rebecca Childer's arms, but Angela met him with a beaming smile.

'You've organised quite a reunion,' he drawled at her.

He wasn't angry. Not really. But he'd geared himself up for seeing Emma at the wedding, not here. Claire had just dropped a bombshell on him which they hadn't had time to talk through, and he probably wasn't going to make it to the wedding now. It left him feeling…out of step somehow.

He hadn't even glimpsed Emma this week, hadn't spoken to her at any length since Lachlan Hancock's birth, and didn't want an unsatisfactory five minutes with her now. He wanted much more, or he wanted nothing. He thought, without having *time* to think, that Claire's decision might have opened a whole new world of possibilities, but did Emma still want any of them, after more than six weeks of awkwardness and silence? And was he at the point where he could ask?

He didn't want to get this wrong. The time they'd spent together weeks ago no longer seemed quite real, after the distance and sense of failure that they'd endured since.

'Yes, well, Susan brought Rebecca and Alethea in, of course, so she's here,' Angela said. 'And then Rebecca had said to me over the phone that if any of Alethea's nurses wanted to see her and were around, she'd love them to come in, too. I didn't want to disturb you again, and I was sure you wouldn't mind, so I made a couple of calls, and here we are.'

She waved an arm around and he saw Sue North and Jane Cameron as well, flanking Emma on each side, although he hadn't even glimpsed them till Angela had mentioned 'nurses'.

'Nell Cassidy's still caught up at the hospital, unfortunately, although I did phone her, too,' Angela added.

'Dr Croft!' Rebecca exclaimed, and Emma looked up at once, giving him an uncertain smile that caught at his heart and tore strips off it. He wouldn't be surprised if she'd moved on in her heart. He'd given her so little— so little shared time to remember, so little of the future to count on.

He came forward, pretending that Alethea was his only focus. 'Is this our little trouper?'

'Would you have recognised her?' Rebecca asked, grinning. She held the baby out to him, and he took her carefully into his arms.

'No, I wouldn't!' he said.

Still small for her age, Alethea nonetheless looked like a real baby now, her bones healthily covered in baby fat. At just over three months, and the veteran of two major operations, each lasting hours and involving, he guessed, around eight or ten highly qualified people, she was awake and alert and smiling.

This was that delightful stage he remembered Jessie and Zoe going through, when a baby's heart belonged to the whole world, and she'd smile at everyone in sight. Alethea had a little fuzz of golden hair beginning to grow, and plump cheeks as smooth and soft and pink as strawberry ice cream, and Rebecca was obviously intensely proud of her.

Also, to be honest, she'd grown used to the attention and the praise for her little heroine. Well, anyone who'd been through what she had deserved to glow and gloat.

'She's gorgeous. She's fabulous,' he told her truthfully.

'She is, Rebecca,' Emma murmured.

Pete held the baby, and the crowd of interested on-lookers pressed Emma close against him. She felt the fuzz of hair on his forearm tickling her own bare skin, and the aura of warmth and strength he so unconsciously and effortlessly gave off.

'She gave us a terrible scare, and she got her picture in several newspapers,' he said, smiling down at the baby, 'But we've forgiven all that now, haven't we, cutie, because you're doing so well!'

Emma tried to focus on the baby. Alethea did her best to be fascinating. She waved her little arms. She dribbled a little from those pink lips with their pale sucking blisters still apparent. She smiled again.

But all I'm really thinking about is Pete.

He had that soft, smiling expression on his face that good men got when they looked at babies, and he radiated a certain pride and satisfaction, too. He'd earned this right, since he'd played such an important part in the successful diagnosis of Alethea's heart condition.

In the weeks Emma had seen so little of him she'd forgotten...*foolishly* forgotten...just what an over-whelming effect he had on her. Just how easily his smile made her heart turn over. Just how much she wanted to touch him, hold him, feel the gift of his body heat wrapped around her, and hear the dark lick of his voice speaking words meant only for her.

She knew she would see him at the wedding tonight, but perhaps she shouldn't have responded to Angela Meredith's phone call just now. It was too hard to see him like this! She could easily have pretended another commitment.

Another patient arrived. Even allowing for those who were here to see Pete's practice partner, Lauren Dempsey, the place was crowded. Pete must be running behind. The wedding was at six, and he was obviously also thinking about how time was passing. He held the baby for another minute, then said to Rebecca and her mother, 'If you have any questions or concerns, please, don't wait. Get on the phone straight away. Even if it seems like just a sniffle or a degree of fever.'

'I will, I promise. Are these all your patients waiting, Dr Croft?' Rebecca asked him.

'Not all of them. But if I don't call the next one in soon, they'll switch doctors and I'll have none! I'd better let you get her home.'

He handed the baby back to her carefully, looked at his watch, then looked at Emma. She couldn't tear her eyes away. He took in a breath, and she waited. She didn't want much. Just a word or two. If he'd been about to say something to her, however, he must have changed his mind. Instead, he turned to the reception desk to pick up his next file.

Sue asked Emma if she wanted to go for a quick coffee, but Emma said no. It took considerable time and effort to do justice to the Paris dress.

And all of it is for Pete, she realised, not for Kit and Gian, as it should be. Which is probably crazy and doomed to disaster, because he didn't say a word about the wedding, or anything else.

Gian and Kit had chosen the rose garden at Kingsford Mill for their ceremony and the large function room there for their reception. At this time of year, a six o'clock garden wedding meant balmy temperatures and late golden sunshine and flowers in bloom. Emma had seated herself with the other guests in time to see Gian striding into position, looking rather on edge and flanked by his brother Marco as best man.

Kit hadn't arrived yet.

Neither had Pete, but his presence wasn't crucial to the event, and Emma tried not to dwell on the fact of his absence. He'd get here soon. How she'd deal with it, she didn't know.

A white car pulled up at the kerb, and here was the bride, with her father to walk her across the grass to the arch of climbing yellow roses where Gian stood, her mother waiting to fuss over her dress and Bonnie to act as an endearingly confused and exuberant flower girl.

Kit looked fabulous, and Gian seemed hardly able to breathe as he gazed at her. Nell sniffled into a handkerchief and muttered darkly about how silly it was to react this way and when would she learn a little good sense? Caroline luxuriated in her teary state, enjoying every second of it, but in between the two of them, Emma stayed dry-eyed.

This lovely wedding didn't make her want to cry, it just settled a hard, hopeless lump deep in her throat, and she hated the way she felt. What, couldn't she enjoy her friend's happiness, purely because one other guest was late?

The civil marriage celebrant pronounced Gian and Kit to be man and wife, and they signed the register. Uniformed waiters served cocktails on the terrace while the bridal couple and their immediate family posed for photographs against the background of blooming roses.

No Pete.

Emma talked to Caroline and Nell and some of the other guests. Caroline's son brought his mother a glass of champagne from a passing waiter's tray and earned a fond squeeze. 'I'd rather you didn't do that in public, Mum,' he told her.

'Isn't he gorgeous?' she said. 'If only there were more men like him!'

'You can give that stuff a rest, too,' he growled, but he was grinning with an endearing mix of awkwardness and pride at the same time.

Everyone moved inside, where a band had begun to play. The three-course meal came in stages, with breaks for dancing, speeches and toasts. The extensive Italian contingent refused to allow this to be a staid occasion. If the atmosphere even hinted that it might fall flat, forks began to tap insistently against glasses, a signal to the bride and groom that they were expected to kiss, and they happily obliged.

No Pete.

Emma knew he wasn't on call. She'd heard his practice partner saying something to Angela about covering this weekend. So why wasn't he here? Kit and Gian must have noticed. They'd probably said something to each other about it. Or perhaps he'd phoned Gian with an explanation. She wasn't going to ask.

He'd looked at her this afternoon in his waiting room. He'd been about to speak. And then he hadn't. Now he wasn't here. No reason to think his absence was anything to do with her. No reason to assume she was that significant in his life any more. Maybe this was why his absence hurt so much. Because she wasn't involved.

The cake arrived, wheeled in on a trolley draped in pristine white cloth. The two-tiered construction was covered in rolled fondant icing and decorated in dark pink ribbon and delicate lace patterns of palest rose. The white satin bow on the knife handle almost hid Kit's hand, and when Gian closed his hand on top, their two sets of fingers made a seamless whole. They pressed down on the knife, and everybody clapped and cheered.

Including Pete.

When had he appeared? Just now, as far as Emma was concerned. He stood on the opposite side of the room, and if he'd seen her, he wasn't looking at her at this moment. She flushed at once from head to toe, and wished she had Caroline and Nell here for camouflage. No, for protection. But they'd moved closer to Kit and Gian, and were talking to Kit's parents.

Now he'd seen her. The band had begun to play again, and couples crowded onto the floor. Pete moved in her direction, his intent so apparent and strong that he only narrowly avoided several collisions with the dancers. Unconsciously, Emma moved toward him, so that when he reached her she was on the dance floor, too.

'Where have you been?' she blurted, unnerved by the way his gaze had fixed on her.

'With Claire.'

Her heart sank. Always with Claire! And what had she been so foolishly hoping? That weddings were contagious, or something? That an expensive gown from Paris would get the perfect romantic scene that it deserved?

'I'm sorry,' he said. 'I wanted to be here. I am here now, at least.' His arms had wound around her, softening her will to resist. 'It was important, though.'

'It always is.' The bitter phrase escaped her lips and soured the shape of her mouth, she could feel it.

'We've solved things now.' He began to pull her into a slow dance, although she scarcely realised she was moving. 'We've realised what was wrong.'

'You're back together,' she guessed aloud. She lifted her chin and nodded brightly, as if she'd been expecting this news, as if it didn't tear her heart open with one agonising slash while her feet twittered to and fro, vaguely in time with his.

He froze.

'No! Hell, no! Not that! I've realised…and Claire has, too…what was stopping us from making any progress with decisions about custody, that's all. All?' He repeated the word. 'It was getting in the way of everything, Emma, and the fact that we've dealt with it now, and understood it…'

'I don't understand, Pete. You'll have to…' she took a jagged, painful breath, and tried to laugh '…speak slowly and in monosyllables, or something. I don't understand what you're saying.'

'She didn't want the girls. That was the problem. She thought she ought to want them, and have them with her, because mothers are supposed to, but she was terrified of it. Zoe broke her arm this afternoon, you see…'

'Oh, no!'

'She's fine. But something suddenly clicked for Claire when she found herself handling the accident so badly, and she understood what's been tearing her up all along. She couldn't handle the girls, so she kept reaching out to me, wanting me in her life in some way to take the pressure off. As soon as she could finally admit it, to herself and to me, the solution was clear. The girls will stay with me, full time and permanently.'

'You won't move?' Emma blurted.

'I won't move. Claire will have them to visit in the holidays, of course, and come and see them for the occasional weekend, but she won't have them with her for any length of time. She never wanted our marriage, not really, even from the beginning. She just wanted me because she was terrified of being a parent alone.'

'That's great, Pete, to get it settled, and to under-stand,' Emma told him, because she knew it was.

He'd been hoping for this for so long—a permanent, workable solution that didn't hurt his darling girls. And she could see in his face how much it meant to him. There was a new clarity in his golden-brown eyes, and the tight little knots at his temples and around his mouth, which she'd thought were a permanent part of the shape of his face, had softened out of existence.

He looked several years younger, and yet at the same time even stronger and more mature. He looked like a man who had the hope of happiness, and who knew he'd earned it...

Until he frowned.

'I won't blame you, though, if you think this has all come too late,' he said.

'Too late?'

'For us, Emma.' Pete searched her face. 'It's been a mess. Terrible timing. Other priorities. I shouldn't have pretended we were just friends. That was a mistake.'

'I pretended it just as much.'

'I was the one who blew the illusion out of the water at the wrong time.'

'Claire's visit spooked me,' she admitted. 'A lot of things spooked me. It always seemed that you were find-ing it too hard to get out of each other's lives, and I wondered if that meant there was something left between you after all, much more than you admitted.'

'No. It was only ever the girls. Only Claire's ambiv-alence, and then the shock of her illness. I've been very clear in my feelings for a long time. First, that our mar-riage was a mistake from the beginning. And lately...' He stopped speaking, and his dance steps slowed.

The band began to play 'Ain't No Sunshine' at a seductively slow tempo, with the lead singer wringing every drop of poignant emotion from the words. Several feet from them, Nell suddenly exclaimed, 'Oh, *God*!' in a choked voice. 'They'd have to play this, of all things, wouldn't they?'

'Nell?' Emma said. She remembered that Nell had always had problems with this song, but typically she had never explained why.

'Leave me alone! This is my problem. Stupid ghosts from the past. Get on with it, you two.' She gave them a pained, upside-down smile. 'I mean it!' She turned abruptly and headed in the direction of the ladies' room.

'Does she?' Pete murmured. 'Mean it, I mean.'

'In that tone, yes.'

'I've always liked this song, actually,' Pete said. His arms tightened around Emma, and he'd stopped even pretending to dance. He was only swaying, and holding her. 'Covers how I've been feeling lately, too. So clear, and so simple. No sunshine when you're gone, Emma. That lovely warmth. That heat.' His mouth brushed hers, making her pulses leap instantly. 'All the sunshine when we're together, and none of it when you're gone. And I want the sunshine. I want you in this dress. Wanted it the day I first saw it. I want you *out* of it, too. And I can offer it now. I can offer you everything you deserve. My heart. My life. My girls to love. If you're still interested, that is.'

'Oh, I'm interested,' Emma said. 'I'm fascinated. I'm eager and ready and— I love you, Pete.'

'I love you, too. Feel what it's doing to me just to say it.' She could. He was holding every muscle so tight he was almost shaking. 'I love you, Emma.' He kissed her sweetly, not caring if anyone was looking on. 'I can't ask you to marry me yet. It wouldn't be fair. It's too

soon, and we both need time. But I'm giving you fair
warning.'

'Oh, yes?'

'Oh, yes! Somewhere a few months down the track,
when you least expect it, probably at sunset, I'm going
to produce a big bunch of roses and go down on my
knees and—'

'Could there be a red Ferrari involved as well, perhaps?' Emma suggested, hugely encouraged by the mention of roses and sunset.

'A red Ferrari?'

'Roaring up my driveway, with you at the wheel.'

'Oh, there could, yes,' he agreed.

'Drowning out the sound of the violins on my stereo.'

'I'm really getting the picture now. There definitely
could.'

'And it might even just happen that I'm wearing this
dress.'

'OK, now you're cheating. I can arrange the red
Ferrari—I'm sure there'll be a luxury car rental place in
Sydney that handles them—but I can't arrange this dress
without tipping you off as to my intentions.'

'Never mind,' Emma said. 'Just kiss me, and we'll
worry about the rest of it later.'

Two months later, as it turned out, on a hot February
Friday, just as the sun had sunk to the horizon and a
cool evening breeze had freshened the air. Emma stood
on her front lawn, wondering why the sprinkler hadn't
come on when she'd turned the tap. Looking along the
hose, she found a kink, and heard, at the same moment,
the throaty growl of an expensive car cruising down her
street.

Not yet having correctly identified the sound, she
glanced up, pulling the hose in her hands to straighten

the kink. Water filled the air around her as the sprinkler spurted into action, drenching her at once and making rainbows of misty spray in the air, just as she caught sight of the car.

Red. Open-topped. Loud. With the familiar shape of a particular man at the wheel, and two little girls shrieking in excitement in the back seat.

With her wet coral pink T-shirt and black bike shorts clinging closer to her body than her Paris dress, Emma began to laugh.

Her future had just roared into the driveway.

Modern Romance™
...seduction and
passion guaranteed

Tender Romance™
...love affairs that
last a lifetime

Medical Romance™
...medical drama
on the pulse

Historical Romance™
...rich, vivid and
passionate

Sensual Romance™
...sassy, sexy and
seductive

Blaze Romance™
...the temperature's
rising

27 new titles every month.

Live the emotion

MILLS & BOON®

MB3

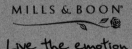

Live the emotion

BIG
CHANGES

We hope you like the new, bigger and better series books this month. Now you can enjoy more of the same great stories—all at the same great prices!

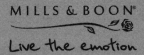

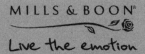

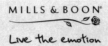

Live the emotion

PENNINGTON

BOOK SEVEN

Available from 2nd January 2004

*Available at most branches of WHSmith, Tesco, Martins, Borders,
Eason, Sainsbury's and most good paperback bookshops.*

PENN/RTL/7

FREE

4 BOOKS
AND A SURPRISE GIFT!

We would like to take this opportunity to thank you for reading this Mills & Boon® book by offering you the chance to take FOUR more specially selected titles from the Medical Romance™ series absolutely FREE! We're also making this offer to introduce you to the benefits of the Reader Service™—

- ★ FREE home delivery
- ★ FREE monthly Newsletter
- ★ FREE gifts and competitions
- ★ Exclusive Reader Service discount
- ★ Books available before they're in the shops

Accepting these FREE books and gift places you under no obligation to buy; you may cancel at any time, even after receiving your free shipment. Simply complete your details below and return the entire page to the address below. *You don't even need a stamp!*

YES! Please send me 4 free Medical Romance books and a surprise gift. I understand that unless you hear from me, I will receive 6 superb new titles every month for just £2.60 each, postage and packing free. I am under no obligation to purchase any books and may cancel my subscription at any time. The free books and gift will be mine to keep in any case.

M3ZED

Ms/Mrs/Miss/Mr ....Initials ....
BLOCK CAPITALS PLEASE

Surname ....

Address ....

....

....Postcode ....

Send this whole page to:
UK: FREEPOST CN81, Croydon, CR9 3WZ
EIRE: PO Box 4546, Kilcock, County Kildare (stamp required)